W9-CDZ-556

THE THINGS A BROTHER KNOWS

THE THINGS A
BROTHER KNOWS

DANA REINHARDT

WENDY
L A M B
BOOKS

Visit us on the Web! www.randomhouse.com/teens
Educators and librarians, for a variety of teaching tools, visit us at
www.randomhouse.com/teachers

Library of Congress Cataloging-in-Publication Data
Reinhardt, Dana.
The things a brother knows / Dana Reinhardt. — 1st ed.
p. cm.
Summary: Although they have never gotten along well, seventeen-year-old Levi follows his older brother Boaz, an ex-Marine, on a walking trip from Boston to Washington, D.C. in hopes of learning why Boaz is completely withdrawn.
ISBN 978-0-375-84455-3 (hc) — ISBN 978-0-375-94455-0 (lib. bdg.) —
ISBN 978-0-375-89762-7 (ebook)
[1. Brothers—Fiction. 2. Soldiers—Fiction. 3. Post-traumatic stress disorder—Fiction. 4. Walking—Fiction. 5. Jews—United States—Fiction. 6. Family life—Massachusetts— Boston—Fiction. 7. Boston (Mass.)—Fiction.] I. Title.
PZ7.R2753Thi 2010
[Fic]—dc22
2009035867

Printed in the United States of America
10 9 8 7 6 5 4 3

First Edition

For Mark Reinhardt and Justin Reinhardt,
my beloved brothers.

THE THINGS A BROTHER KNOWS

ONE

I USED TO LOVE MY BROTHER.

Now I'm not so sure.

That's a terrible thing to say. Believe me, I know it. I wouldn't ever say it out loud to anybody, not even Pearl. Especially since everyone else loves him. Even the people who've never met him. They can't get enough of him. They worship him.

I used to worship him too. All little brothers worship their big brothers, I guess. It sort of goes with the job description. Think about it. Your brother's face is one of the first you ever see. His hands are among the first to touch you. You crawl only to catch him. You want nothing but to walk like he does, talk like he does, draw a picture, throw a ball, tell a joke like he does, let loose one of those crazy whistles with four fingers jammed in your mouth or burp the ABCs just like he does. To your little mind, he's got the whole of the world all figured out.

But then you grow up. You start thinking for yourself. You make your own decisions and those decisions change you, and they can even change the people around you, and my brother made one big whopper of a decision, and in the end, it's made it really hard for me to love him anymore.

And I feel like shit about it. Really, I do. But what can I say? It's how I feel.

He's coming home. Sometime tonight.

Everyone knows it.

For one thing, they made an announcement at morning assembly. So that's how my day started.

Even though Mr. Bowers never said my name, and even if there were people there who didn't know about Boaz, how many dudes have the last name Katznelson? Our Boston suburb isn't exactly packed with relocated Israelis.

So when Bowers said, "We all, each and every one of us, owe a personal debt of gratitude to Boaz Katznelson, a graduate of this very school, who returns tonight from three years as a marine, and who has served this country at great personal sacrifice." I was pretty sure people were staring at me.

I pulled the brim of my Red Sox cap down low over my face. A smattering of applause echoed off the gym walls.

"He could have chosen any sort of future he wanted. I know this is hard for some of you seniors to imagine, but any college would have taken him. He was, in every way, a superlative student. But he chose duty. He chose to serve our great nation in this very difficult and very challenging time of war."

At this point there were a few hisses and muffled boos. I felt random hands slap my shoulders and back.

I typically start my mornings in the courtyard with Zim, comparing notes on the homework we blew off, sipping coffee from 7-Eleven and eating mini doughnuts. The kind we eat are so fake they're not doughnuts—they're "do-nuts"—which makes you wonder what's really in them. But anyway, this morning was a weird one. Like the day didn't already promise to be weird enough.

Zim caught up with me after the assembly.

"You okay?"

Zim and I share a birthday. He moved in across the street when we were both seven years, eight months and eleven days old. I'd say he was my best friend if there weren't a Pearl in my life.

"Yeah. I guess so."

"Cool, man. I'll catch you later. I'm pretty sure my mom's cooking something inedible to bring by your place tonight. Seriously, whatever it is, it reeks. Proceed with caution."

"Will do."

"And Levi?"

"Yeah?"

"I'm glad he's coming home."

"Yeah. Me too," I said, because of course I'm glad he's coming home. I'm glad he's okay. *Glad* doesn't really do it. I'm thrilled, relieved, ecstatic, whatever. I'd say a prayer of thanks, if I were that sort of person, that my brother is returning from this war I don't believe in. This war I can't understand. This war for which nobody should have given up so much, and hurt so many people, and worried his mother down to a sack of bones.

But this was his choice. And we've all lived with it ever since.

Look, I know how this makes me sound. Like a whiner. Some sort of self-pitying wuss. And yes, on some level, that's who I am. But I'm not only talking about me here. I'm talking about my family, about how we used to be before he left and who we all are now. And I'm talking about what he's been like those few times he's made it back home: how he shuts himself in his room and doesn't say a word. I'm talking about the letters he failed to send.

Maybe I sound even worse than self-pitying: un-American or anti-American. That's a tight spot to be in for a guy with a weird Israeli last name and a father with a thick accent who makes me call him Abba instead of Dad like we all still live in Israel, but I'm neither of those things. I'm not un or anti. I just don't know what to think about this whole big mess we're in.

And who knows. Maybe that's even worse than being un or anti, because at least then you know where you stand.

When I get home from school it's an afternoon like any other since he's been gone. Nothing elaborate cooking on the stove. No streamers, banners or hand-painted signs. No champagne in the fridge. Not even a cake.

I go up to my room. Lie down on the floor. Pull out my iPod and put *Abbey Road* on shuffle. I stare at my feet. I heard someplace I can't remember, but probably from Zim because he's a wealth of totally useless knowledge, that if your second toe is longer than your first, you're twice as likely to reach a position of power in your life.

Abba asked me to empty the rain gutters after school. He

didn't ask, he barked. That's Abba's way. But I'm sitting on the floor, staring at my long first toe, and how it dwarfs my second.

Mom is downstairs cleaning, filling the house with the smell of fake spring. This is how she spends her days. Wiping, polishing, folding, straightening. She hums as she cleans. Tuneless, shapeless humming.

I know enough about Mom and her superstitions to have predicted that no celebration would be under way. Not until he walks in the front door and closes it behind him. You don't spill salt on the table without throwing some over your shoulder. You don't let an object come between you and someone else without saying "Bread and butter." You don't place a hat on the bed. And you never celebrate your good fortune until it's real enough that you can hold it in your hands or clutch it to your chest.

I offered to go pick him up. I figured that would be a shock. Boaz has been gone since before I earned my learner's permit. Now I'm fully licensed, with two parking tickets and a citation for a rolling stop to prove it.

I saw the whole scene playing out on this little movie screen in my head. I imagined pulling up to a curb somewhere. Boaz would be standing outside, a duffel thrown over his shoulder. I would roll down the passenger-side window and say something like "Need a lift?" It would be evening, but still, I saw myself with sunglasses, never mind that I don't own any. I imagined a slow smile spreading across my brother's stony face.

Maybe we'd shake hands. Or slap each other on the back. Then I'd drive him home.

But imagining is just that. And anyway, Abba said no, that Boaz had his own plans for his return and I should just go on about my business.

So that's what I'm doing. And my business does not involve cleaning the rain gutters when there is no hint of rain.

I'm waiting. I'm always waiting. My family is always waiting. For something, some word, some news, some event to change everything. But I'm starting to think that maybe today it's not such a crazy thing to wait. Maybe change is coming, finally. Maybe he'll come back and it'll be like it was before he left.

Then I think of John Lennon, the one true love of my life. It's a hero-worship sort of love, not the gay sort of love that Pearl and Zim like to tease me about. I think of the line from "Beautiful Boy." *Life is what happens to you while you're busy making other plans.* Right. And change is what happens when you aren't sitting on your bedroom floor, staring at your toes, waiting for it to come.

Change creeps in quietly. It grows like hair or fingernails. It spreads through you slowly, like the dull ache you get in your cheeks when you've been faking a smile too long.

I stretch out and roll onto my stomach. I close my eyes. The rumble of Mom's vacuum is having a lulling effect on me. Lots of stuff does that. Airplanes, the backseats of cars, chemistry class.

A nap. Naps are always good. I assume the position of sleep—arms tucked under me, legs spread out, head to the left. I dig my cheek deeper into the plush carpeting.

My door flies open.

Pearl never believed much in knocking.

"Ooops. So sorry. Were you having a little private Levi time?"

I pull out my ear buds. "No."

She throws her backpack on my bed and kicks off her shoes. "I meant the 'little private Levi time' thing as a euphemism. Masturbating. Get it?"

"I got it."

"Maybe it would have been funnier if I'd said 'some private time with Little Levi.' "

"Nope."

She lies down next to me and stares up at the ceiling.

"So what are we doing on the floor?"

"I dunno."

Pearl has arrived straight from school, still in her uniform. She goes to the Convent of the Holy Child Jesus, and as if that weren't tough enough, try going to a Catholic girls' school when you're Jewish. And Chinese.

We met in Hebrew school. She used to make fun of me for being short and skinny. Nobody had ever bothered to tease me before, not even my brother, and I sort of liked it. And her. Eventually, she came around to liking me too.

She wanted us to form a band. A pop rock duo.

"We'll be the new John and Yoko," she said.

"But Pearl, Yoko was *Japanese*."

"Like you know the difference."

It might have worked out if either of us knew how to play an instrument. Or carry a tune.

Pearl picks herself up off the floor and offers me a hand.

"C'mon. I need a smoke."

She still hasn't forgiven me for quitting. She takes it as a personal affront.

We climb out the window and assume our usual perch on the roof. It's late spring and the air is heavy with heat.

She holds the pack out in my direction. "Want one?"

"Are you ever going to stop asking me that?"

"Nope."

She lights up a Marlboro.

"You know, Levi, this whole not smoking thing, it just makes you boring. I mean, without it, where's your edge?" She blows a thick plume of smoke right into my face. "You, my friend, are currently edgeless."

Once, during P.E., they brought in this yoga teacher, and they made us all do these weird stretches and stupid breathing exercises, but it wasn't half bad for me because (a) I was sitting right behind Rebecca Walsh and that girl is seriously limber, and (b) when the teacher had us close our eyes, and she led us through these mental exercises involving lapping waves and calm breezes and asked us to imagine our "safe place," and told us to go there in our minds, I wound up right here on this particular slab of roof, sitting next to Pearl.

This is my safe place.

I say this even though the slope is pretty steep, and today I imagine, on that movie screen in my head, what it might feel like to lose my balance. To slide right off. To disappear over the rain gutter jammed with too many leaves.

If I fell, I'd land on the brick patio. And that wouldn't feel so great.

Boaz put in that brick patio. He knows how to do stuff like that. I remember the smell of the cement. The way it dried under my fingernails after I ignored his warning and slipped my hands into the bucket while it was still wet.

Pearl lies back and puts her arms behind her head. She speaks out of the side of her mouth that isn't holding the cigarette.

"Wanna catch a movie later? There's nothing I want to see, but the guy selling popcorn is seriously hot."

"I don't like popcorn."

"So I'll buy you some Milk Duds."

"Milk Duds hurt my teeth."

"So how about some—"

"Pearl. I can't go to the movies."

"Fine. Be that way."

Pearl knows this afternoon isn't really like other afternoons. Everyone knows. But she's not trying to engage me in any sort of deep conversation about my feelings or whatever, because Pearl is a halfway decent friend.

It's been thirteen months.

That's the last time he came home.

He must have had some breaks in there somewhere, some leave time. But he chose to do something else with those breaks, and we don't know what it was, or who he was with, or where he went, because somewhere along the road he'd decided that communication with the family he left behind wasn't a priority.

Pearl cocks her head and narrows her eyes at me from behind her square-framed glasses. "Do you want to get out of here? Come over to my house for dinner? Mama Goldblatt is making a tuna casserole. Our house smells like a pet store."

One thing, and there aren't many, that Pearl and Zim have in common is that they both wear the wretchedness of their mothers' cooking like some sort of badge of honor. But for all that Mom's gone through these past three years, she's still a great cook, which may be why my friends hang around my house for dinner so often. It sure can't have anything to do with the cheery atmosphere.

I take in a greedy breath of Pearl's secondhand smoke.

"I'd love to, really, but I think my attendance is mandatory here tonight."

She reaches out and steps on my foot with her own. I hadn't even noticed I was jiggling it like a toddler with a hyperactivity disorder.

"Levi. It's gonna be okay."

"How do you know?"

"I don't. It's just one of those things friends are supposed to say to each other. I'm just trying to do my job here."

"Well, thanks."

We climb back in through the window and I head downstairs in search of caffeine. Without cigarettes it's all I have left.

Mom's in the living room folding laundry. Organizing the piles into perfectly lined rows. I don't remember her always being such a neat freak, but sometimes it's hard to sort out the then from the now.

Then she was a stay-at-home mom who did freelance graphic design out of her little office in the garage. *Now* she does much more of the staying home and less of the graphic design.

She's been on edge for the last three years, and she likes to say that cleaning is to her what golf is to businessmen. It relaxes her.

If that's true, I'd hate to see what she'd be like without all the laundry.

"Here you go, baby." She hands me a stack of folded T-shirts.

I've always hated when Mom calls me *baby*. Boaz never seemed to mind. And anyway, it's nearly impossible for anyone to infantilize my brother.

I'm a different story. Until pretty recently, I was waging an uphill battle on the road to manhood. I still have hair to my shoulders, but that's by choice. Luckily the height and weight issues are finally starting to sort themselves out. I'm probably five nine now if I'd stand up straight, and at long last, I think I weigh more than Zim's dog.

But I've never laced up my boots to fight in some desert country half a world away.

I don't even own any boots.

When I really think about it, I guess what burns most about hearing my mother calling me baby is the sad truth that nobody ever calls me baby but my mother.

I think about telling her to stop. That no self-respecting seventeen-year-old goes around getting called baby by his mother. But she smiles at me right then, just barely, and I don't have it in me to dash the look of fake hope on her face that is the perfect companion to the smell of spring in a spray bottle.

She deserves this moment, right? She deserves to stand here folding her laundry. Not allowing the anticipation and excitement to overwhelm her, but still smiling, just a little, knowing that tonight, her son is finally coming home.

It's good news. There's no two ways about it. It's great news. It's the best news any mother folding laundry in any living room in any town in this or any country could ever possibly hope for. But I don't know which son she's thinking of. The one who left three years ago, or the one he's become while he's been gone.

I take the shirts from her outstretched hands. "Thanks, Mom." I start to walk away and then stop. "Anything you need me to do?"

My question shocks us both, I think. Me, because I can't remember the last time I offered to do anything around the house, and Mom, because of all the days to change things up, today is not the day. She's tethered to her routine by a very fine thread.

"No thanks, baby."

I reach into her row of piles for the stack of cloud sheets. Boaz's room still has the same aviator theme she designed for him when he was little. She painted the airplanes on the walls herself. Hung the planets from the ceiling.

She did my walls with starfish, clown fish, hammerhead sharks and an octopus. That octopus scared the crap out of me. I was that kind of kid. Scared of an octopus, but even more scared to admit it to anybody. Pearl and I painted over my walls four years ago in a color she picked out called November Rain.

"Are you going to put these sheets on his bed?" I ask.

She pats the pile tenderly and then worries a corner of the top sheet between her fingertips. "Bo always did love these sheets."

We call him Boaz. Everyone does. Boaz, my parents say, is a good Hebrew name. It means "swiftness," "strength." They always fought the impulse most people had to Americanize it. But a month or so into his service, letters started arriving home signed *Bo*.

Then they stopped arriving altogether.

Now I say, "You want me to do it for you?"

A puzzled look.

"Put the sheets on his bed. I can do it if you want."

She waves me off. "No, no. It's okay." She returns to her folding. Her humming.

And I return upstairs to Pearl with my caffeine.

She's searching through my closet. Pearl likes to steal my clothes. A car pulls into the driveway and she freezes with a worn-out flannel shirt in her grip.

It isn't Abba. He came home half an hour ago to ride me about not cleaning the gutters.

My heart beats sharply. Like it might slice its way right through my chest.

I go to the window and lean out.

The light is just leaving the sky, but I can still make out the trunk of Dov's lime-green Caprice Classic. It's the car I learned to drive in. Boaz too, although he somehow managed to look cool behind its gargantuan steering wheel. It takes three full rotations just to make a right turn in Dov's Caprice Classic. I figure I'm as prepared to captain a boat now as I am to drive a car.

Dov is seventy-six years old, with a face like a rumpled suit, untamable white hair and sideburns he's had for so long they've finally come back in style. Nearly two decades of living in the States has done nothing to soften his matter-of-fact Israeli gruffness. There's nothing soft about Dov—no soft edges, no softer sides. He's built like a badass garden gnome.

Dov has been coming for dinner at least three times a week since Boaz enlisted. He always arrives with the *New York Times* folded under his arm, but he never talks about the war anymore. He'll take to his favorite chair in the living room, the red suede armchair, and he'll carry on about drilling in the Arctic. The riots in France. The section of Interstate 90 that's closed due to a crumbling overpass.

"Can you believe this mess? What a *shande*!"

Lately, he could even work himself up over a game of baseball.

He knocks. Loud.

"C'mon in, Dov."

Sometimes grandfathers choose to go by their first names because they think *Grandpa* makes them sound old, but not Dov. "I know I'm an old son of a bitch," he'd say. "That's why I don't want some little *pischer* calling me anything new. All these years now, I'm used to my name."

Abba calls him Dov too. As a boy growing up in Israel, he never had the chance to call his father Abba. That's why he chose to be an Abba himself instead of a Dad like all the other fathers all over this country.

Dov doesn't move any farther into the room than the doorway.

"Good evening, Miss Pearl." He's crazy for Pearl.

"Hiya, Dov."

"Will you tell your friend here to get a haircut?"

My long hair is a subject of which Dov never seems to tire.

Pearl shrugs. "Get a haircut, Levi."

I go over and give Dov a hug.

"You look like a lady," he says as he gives me a few good pats on my back. Then he leans back and looks me over. He squeezes my cheek. "A pretty lady. I'll give you that."

Dov joined the army when he turned eighteen, but he'd be the first to tell you it was different from what Boaz did. Everyone in Israel serves in the army. Abba did. Even my grandmother did. It's what you do when you turn eighteen. There's no choice, so joining the army doesn't make you brave or crazy. It doesn't turn you into a hero or a freak. It doesn't make you somebody who has something to prove.

It only makes you just like everybody else.

Dov goes downstairs and Pearl starts packing her things.

My phone rings. I don't even have to look to know it's Zim. If Pearl is standing in front of me there's only one person who could possibly be on the other end of this call.

I hit Speaker.

"Yo."

"Yo."

" 'Sup?"

" 'Sup?"

"Wow," Pearl says. "What scintillating conversationalists you gentlemen are."

"*She's* there?"

Zim and Pearl have a little healthy competition going on about who's my better friend, a ridiculous sort of contest when you consider the prize.

"Hello, Richard." Pearl calls Zim by his real name just to get under his skin. And Zim retaliates by pretending the only reason I hang out with Pearl is because we're having sex. Which is, just to be clear, totally not true.

"So I don't want to interrupt whatever unmentionable acts you two are up to, but I just thought Levi should know that none other than Sophie Olsen, hottie extraordinaire, came up to me after third period and asked if he was related to the guy Bowers talked about at morning assembly."

"So?"

"So? Dude. She knows who you are. And she knows enough about who you are to know that you're friends with me. And I don't mean to build you up just to tear you down, but that's about as exciting as news gets in your social world."

Can't argue with that.

When Pearl takes off, I settle into a game of chess with Abba. We play pretty regularly, and pretty regularly he gives me a good whupping. It's how we spend time together without having to actually talk.

A few minutes into the game I hear the front door open. Pearl always leaves something behind. Her sweater, her backpack, her cell phone. Once she even managed to forget her shoes.

Then I hear a voice.

Hello?

It takes an extra beat to reach me, like it's coming from the bottom of a well. My brother's voice.

It's a hesitant *hello*, like the speaker isn't quite sure he's stepped into his own house.

Mom reaches him first. She hasn't bothered to change from her afternoon of cleaning, and she throws her arms around him. Abba and I get up; Dov runs in from the kitchen. We all stand around him, well, *them* really, because from the way she's holding on to him, it's hard to tell where Mom ends and Boaz begins. We stand around grabbing for some part of him, even if only to touch the cuff of his jacket. I feel Dov's grip on my shoulder. We gather in a huddle.

And then, slowly, wordlessly, we cave in on each other, seized by a relief so deep it renders us boneless.

And in this moment I'm able to imagine what we look like from the outside. *Soldier Returns to Loving Embrace of Family.*

In this moment, we are that image.

In this moment, I allow myself to believe that everything will go back to the way it used to be. He has returned.

We have returned.

TWO

HE DOESN'T COME OUT of his room for three days.

In a way, I can relate. There have been times when I wished I could shut my door and never open it again, except to let in Pearl. Or Zim.

"What's he doing in there?" Zim asks me in the courtyard before first period. He's got do-nut powder on his cheek. I'd reach out to wipe it off, but people at school probably already think we're a couple.

"I don't know."

"Geez."

"Yeah."

"Remember that time he took us skateboarding? In that emptied-out swimming pool? And the lady whose house it was came chasing after us with a mop?"

"Yeah."

"A mop! With a sponge at the end!"

He's laughing now and powder is flying out of his mouth.

"That was awesome," he says.

"Yeah, it was."

"Can I come see him? I mean, he used to be kind of like a

big brother to me too, you know? He sort of taught me how to be one."

Zim's little brother, Peter, is Mini Zim, except that he's really chubby.

"You're a better big brother than he is, Zim."

Zim looks at me like I'm crazy, and I hate to see this look coming from him. I know I'm not supposed to say stuff like that, and I'd like to think it's okay to say it to Zim, that he understands, but even he doesn't.

It's not like Boaz was a bad brother. He never tied me to a tree in my underwear or shaved off one of my eyebrows or any of those sorts of things. He taught me how to do some stuff, like how to draw optical illusions and how to give the perfect middle finger. He bought me a book about the Beatles once and it wasn't even my birthday. There was the day he got his driver's license and he came home from the test with Mom and he raced right to my room and asked me, all excited, where I wanted to go.

Anywhere, he said. *I'll take you.*

The North End, I answered. I picked the farthest place I could think of, an Italian neighborhood in Boston, right at the ocean's edge. I was twelve. All I wanted was to be alone with my brother. And maybe get an ice cream.

The North End, he said. *You got it.* And I went for my jacket. In the time it took me to grab it, the phone rang. It was a friend of his, I don't remember who. He turned to me, and looked at the jacket in my hand, and said he was sorry but we'd have to go to the North End tomorrow. And we didn't.

So Zim is looking at me like I'm crazy. But he doesn't see, because he can't. Even if we share a birthday and even if he is one of my two best friends, he can't know what it's been like to be Boaz's younger brother.

Just then Sophie Olsen walks by.

"Hi, Levi," she says. And she gives this little wave.

"Life," Zim says under his breath, "is so totally unfair."

When I get home from school, and I'm sitting on the floor of my room, I hear the toilet flush. Not your typical earth-shattering event, but today it comes as confirmation.

He's alive in there.

Our rooms share a bathroom. He used to lock my door from the inside and then leave it like that, and it used to drive me crazy, because there I'd be, dying for a piss, locked out of my own bathroom. So I'd pound on his door, and he'd have that locked too. He'd say in this high-pitched voice, *Who is it?* like it was some big mystery, and then he'd make me go through this whole round of questions before he'd agree to go back and unlock my door.

When I hear the flushing it occurs to me that I could probably open my door—I'd bet he's forgotten about the lock—and pretend I didn't know anyone was in there. I could make some lame excuse about how all that time having the bathroom to myself, I'd forgotten how to share. That might lead somewhere, to something resembling a conversation.

But I just wait for the sound of his door closing.

I mean, it's not like nobody's trying. Mom knocks. Several times a day. She cheerfully calls out, *Boaz? Honey? Bo?*

He shouts back, *I'm sleeping.*

Not that I've never wanted to shout at Mom like that. Sure I have. In the days before I had a phone with an alarm feature, Mom used to have to wake me for school. She'd pull the shades and sing a little song.

Wake-ee-up-ee-oo-my-little-Levi . . .

I wanted to grab something and hurl it at her.

But I didn't. And Boaz does. This is just what he's doing when he uses that voice with Mom. He's hurling something her way, something heavy enough to hurt her.

He never used to use that voice with her. He used to be affectionate. He'd hug her or hold her hand in public long after I'd be caught dead doing either. He called her "Ma."

I can see how it hurts now as she walks down the hall, but then she'll perk up, because after all, he's home. And home holed up in his room all day not talking or eating beats being thousands and thousands of miles away, in danger's path. Not writing or calling.

Abba's about to blow. He's not as patient or understanding as Mom. Or maybe the operative word is *clueless.*

This morning, he slammed his fist on the breakfast table.

"Benzona!"

I love it when he swears in Hebrew. It never sounds like anything all that bad. For example, to my ear, *benzona* sounds like an Italian pastry. But then I'll go look it up online.

What he'd just said, in the presence of my mother, was "Son of a whore." And he said this while he was looking up at the ceiling, at Boaz's room. So . . . he'd just called Mom someone who has sex for money. Which was kind of uncalled for. I mean, the woman just made him an egg-white omelet, for Christ's sake.

Fortunately, I don't think she ever bothers to translate.

Abba ran his hands through his thinning hair. "When is he going to come down? He can't stay up there forever."

"He just needs a little rest, Reuben. That's all."

Sometimes I forget he's home. I'll be in class staring at the back of Rebecca Walsh's silky hair, or in line at the cafeteria, or home watching TV, or in bed, or out on the roof, and I'll forget.

Then I'll remember. Boaz is home.

And I feel like a shitty brother for the forgetting.

It's Friday night. Shabbat.

I hear the buzz of his electric clippers and then the shower in our bathroom.

Dov's coming for dinner and Boaz must finally be planning on coming downstairs. I think he knows if he didn't, Dov would break down his door and seriously kick his ass.

Dinner is something we were never allowed to skip back when the normal rules applied. We always came home in time for dinner.

It's Abba's thing, dinner is, even if he never does the cooking. He believes in it as much as he believes in anything. He grew up on a kibbutz, and while he claims to have enjoyed the communal life—the freedom, the constant stream of barefoot children chasing after balls that belonged to the lot of them—he missed sitting down to a family dinner. Most often he ate in the dining hall with his friends, and while this sounds like heaven to me, it left Abba with some sort of hole in him it's our job to fix.

Tonight the house is full of the smell of Mom's roasting chicken.

Dov never arrives empty-handed. He's brought some food from the Armenian. That's what he calls the little deli in his neighborhood. The owner, Mr. Kurjian, is the closest thing Dov's got to a friend.

"Give me whatever's good," he says and hands Mr. Kurjian his empty basket.

Today it's stuffed grape leaves, some pizzalike flat bread with spices, and a white cheese that's too runny to cut with a knife.

"Try this," Dov says as I help him lay his goods out on the table. "It's nice and salty."

Abba walks in and they launch into Hebrew.

I pour myself a root beer. Take my time collecting ice cubes, lingering in front of the open freezer door. I try to pick out a word, a phrase, anything familiar. All those Sundays trapped in Hebrew school. Did I really learn nothing?

Then I give up. I should just be glad they're talking instead of pretending like Mom does. I can tell by the pitch of their voices that they know Boaz is not just catching up on sleep. That he isn't going to open up his bedroom door, give a big stretch, rub his eyes and then snap to, like a bear in striped pajamas from an old black-and-white cartoon.

When Boaz finally does come downstairs we all stop and stare. It's just what I told myself I wouldn't do, but none of us can help it. Mom fills the silence.

"Bo, honey, do you want a drink? A slice of cheese? A carrot stick?"

She reaches out and rubs his shaved head like he's a little boy.

His T-shirt hugs his chiseled chest. The tendons in his neck mean business. He hasn't lost any touch of the desert sun on his empty face.

He walks over to Dov, sticking out his hand. They shake like buddies meeting in a bar after work.

We sit around the table.

Mom takes a sip of her wine. "We're so blessed."

Dov rolls his eyes. After Boaz left, Mom started going to synagogue almost every Saturday morning. It used to be she went only on the High Holidays, dragging Boaz and me along, but now Mom is Temple Beth Torah's most reliable attendee. She'd go Friday nights too if she could, but that would get in the way of family dinners, and there's no way Abba would stand for eating potluck style in the synagogue social hall.

Dov starts a rant about the economy. The price of chocolate bars at the Stop & Shop has gone up twice in the past six months. Not that Dov even eats chocolate, but he notices these things, and this is his proof that the economy is on the fast track to hell.

Mom used to call Boaz the Human Hoover, and he's living up to his old name. It's good to see him eating like that again, even if it's only because he's been starving himself for days. And it's easy to explain away his silence when his mouth is full of food.

He approaches his plate with absolute concentration.

Dividing the chicken from the vegetables from the potatoes. He eats them separately, and completely. He leaves nothing behind.

"Boaz. *Nu?*" Abba says because he can't help himself. He can't let it be enough that Boaz is sitting at the table, that he's eating, that he's finally come downstairs.

Boaz looks up from his plate and meets Abba's eyes but doesn't say a thing.

"What's next, son?"

Silence. Only the sound of forks clinking china.

Finally Boaz shrugs. "Back to sleep."

He stands and takes his plate into the kitchen. Mom shoots Abba a *why can't you lay off him* look. Like if Abba had just let Dov rattle on about his chocolate bars all night, everything would be right with the world.

He comes back into the dining room, wiping his hands on his jeans.

"Well," he says. "Good night."

It's seven-thirty.

He turns to leave.

"Bo, honey," Mom pleads. "Sit awhile. I'll get you a cup of tea. Some nice, hot tea."

He shakes his head, then walks slowly over to her and gives her a quick kiss on the cheek before going back upstairs. She beams, electrified.

I'm pretty sure it means nothing. It's what we always do before going to bed. It's a reflex. It doesn't mean Boaz is anywhere closer to acting like himself.

Nobody says anything for a long time.

Maybe I should be sitting here thinking about Boaz. But I'm not. I'm plotting how to make my exit.

I'm supposed to be going to a party at Chad Post's house. I worry about how it looks going off to a party when my brother has just returned from the desert, but I also worry about Zim and Pearl killing me if I bail.

And anyway, if I stayed in tonight, Boaz wouldn't come out of his room. So what's the difference?

It's not like we ever spent our Friday nights hanging out.

We weren't like those brothers who confide in each other, or seek out each other's approval, or commiserate about their parents. We weren't even like those brothers who wrestle or shove each other or pin each other to the floor, laughing so hard they almost puke, hiding their deep affection under a layer of physicality. We were more or less strangers.

Or maybe that's not really fair. I guess I'm talking mostly about what happened when he got to high school. Before that, before he got his driver's license and a girlfriend, there were times I was the only game in town. On vacations we'd build elaborate sand castles or take borrowed bikes and go exploring. One regular Saturday night we watched the whole Godfather trilogy and we didn't even start until ten.

As he got older he sort of gave up on me. He dove into a new world and shut me out. And then he went off to Israel for a summer and came back with the idea that he needed to join the Marines and then all hell broke loose around here.

If he talked to me more, I'd have some idea about why. But I never really understood all that much about him other than that he was stronger, faster, bigger, smarter and way better-looking than me. He had a confidence I marveled at and a girlfriend I fantasized about. Boaz knew what he wanted and he went out and got it. I've never really wanted much of anything.

I'm not so sure how much has changed in the years since he's been gone. I've grown taller and I'm grateful for every quarter inch, but I still don't know what it is I'd give up everything for the way he did, or if such a thing even exists for me.

When I was younger, I used to sneak into his room. I'd run my fingers over his trophies, his collection of rocks, the spines of his books. I thought of myself as somehow stepping into my future. I was catching a glimpse of who I'd become four years down the road.

But in the end that room taught me nothing.

"Levi," Dov turns to me. "Why do you smell so pretty?"

"Because I showered?"

"No. It's more than that."

Dov's right. I put on some cologne. It's been in the medicine cabinet since Boaz's high school days, and I'm taking a leap it hasn't turned toxic. Once I'm bothering with this party I might as well make an effort.

Pearl is tagging along with Zim and me, as per usual.

"It's one of the only benefits of having you as a friend," she says. "They don't know how to throw a party at Convent of the Holy Child Jesus. All those stereotypes about wild Catholic girls aren't true."

"I'm going to a party," I say finally. "I won't be back too late."

I'm not sure why I hesitated. I mean, I can pretty much do

as I please. One benefit of having a brother who chooses a life in a combat zone is that my parents never get all knotted up about where I'm going, or what I'm doing, or who I'm with, or if I'm getting good grades, or how I'll spend my summer vacation, or where I'm applying to college.

They used to bug Boaz about those things and look where that got them.

Dov puts his hand on mine. "Have a good time, beautiful," he says. "And whatever you do, don't forget your handbag."

Pearl is sporting some serious cleavage.

"Mama Goldblatt let you out of the house in *that?*"

She holds up a gray cardigan. "There's a reason God invented sweaters."

She climbs into the back of Zim's car, leans forward and buries her nose in my neck. "You smell yummy."

Zim puts his hand up like he's shielding his eyes from the blinding blaze of a too-close sun. "Gross. Get a room."

She breathes in deeper. "You smell like Boaz used to smell."

I push her away. "Are you for real?"

"I'm a girl. I have a strong olfactory sense. Or maybe it's a Chinese thing. Either way, I remember how he used to smell." She takes one final whiff of me and then falls back into her seat. "Mmmmmmmmmm. The scent of falling in love."

It never occurred to me Pearl might have had a crush on my brother. That was stupid.

I scratch at my neck. Maybe I overdid it with the cologne.

"Okay, you two, remind me why we're going to this party?" I ask. "Chad Post is kind of a tool."

"Because you need to loosen up, Levi," Pearl says. "Get your mind off things. Maybe you can even get somebody to touch your winkle."

"Like you're not all over that daily," Zim snorts.

"Don't call it my winkle," I tell Pearl.

"Don't get bogged down in semantics when we should be working on strategy."

"The girl does have a point," Zim says.

Okay, my experience with the opposite sex is pitiful when you stack it up next to Pearl's or Zim's. But like I said, the last year or so has been good to me physically. Things should get better from here on out.

"What sort of strategy do you suggest?" I ask.

"Well, you could just get some poor girl rip-roaring drunk," Pearl says. "But that's cliché. And morally questionable." She rolls down her window and lights up a cigarette in flagrant violation of Zim's rules for his car. "We'll have to come up with something."

At Chad's Pearl flirts with a guy way out of her league. She loses interest and begins all over again with a science fiction nerd.

Zim disappears with Maddie Green, which is something he does at roughly four out of every five parties, but he swears she's not his girlfriend.

I wander around, skirting the fringes of conversations. Keeping one eye open for Rebecca Walsh, even though she never goes anywhere without Dylan Fredricks.

Chad Post grabs my shoulder.

"Dude," he says. "I heard about your brother."

"Thanks," I say. Then I cringe. Why'd I say *thanks?*

"You must be so psyched to have him home."

He doesn't leave his room and he can't put together a sentence of more than three words.

"Yeah. I am."

"How's he doing?"

Did I mention that he doesn't leave his room and can't put together a sentence of more than three words?

"Great."

"Cool," Chad says. "Wanna beer?"

"Sure."

As Chad heads for the keg, I feel guilt creeping up. I called Chad Post a tool, but maybe he's not so bad.

He returns with a blue plastic cup. He stands next to me, checking out the scene.

"Boaz is so badass," he says, and then he leans in a little closer. He smells like Doritos. "Do you think he killed anybody over there?"

"I don't really know, Chad."

"Well, I think it's awesome what he did. I'm not saying I'd do it myself, 'cause I don't wanna, like, wake up before the sun and eat crappy food and sleep in a tent and get blown up, but I totally respect the guys who do."

"I'll pass that on."

"Awesome. Tell him thanks for keeping our country safe from terrorists and shit."

"I'll do that."

Chad wanders off, and I look around for a place to sit. I'm hoping for a spot where nobody will bother me, unless, of course, that person is Rebecca Walsh. Or Sophie Olsen.

I settle into one half of a love seat.

I pick up a back issue of *Time* magazine and try to look interested. There's a soldier on the cover. Helmet. Desert fatigues. Tired, dusty face. Deep tan.

Pearl squeezes in next to me.

"Way to go. Reading. That'll woo the ladies."

She takes a long sip of my lukewarm beer. "Where's Richard?"

"Where do you think?"

"Maddie Green? So predictable."

"If I didn't know any better, I'd say you sound jealous."

"Please. What about you? How's Project Winkle coming along?"

I gesture to the empty space around me.

"You need to work on strategy," she says.

"Don't you ever get tired of hitting on people?" I ask her. "It looks like an awful lot of work."

"I don't get this opportunity every day, you know. Mama Goldblatt robbed me of my God-given right to flirt by sending me to the Convent."

Mama Goldblatt adopted Pearl when she was eleven months old, and since the day she stepped off the plane as a single mother with that baby in her arms, Mama Goldblatt has been wildly overprotective—there's no other way to account for her sending a Chinese Jew to an all-girls Catholic school. She claims it's because she believes in single-sex education, but I think if she knew Pearl would go ahead and lose her virginity at sixteen anyway, she might have saved herself the tuition and sent her to the public school like everybody else.

"Where'd you tell your mom you were going tonight?"

"I just said I was hanging out with you." Pearl throws her arm around my neck. "Mama Goldblatt never worries when I'm with you. You're safe."

"Great. Safe."

"What? You'd rather be dangerous?"

I put the magazine on the coffee table. Right back where I found it.

I sink deeper into the love seat.

"I'm not sure what I want to be."

THREE

I'M STARTING TO WONDER if he ever sleeps at all.

His radio's on all the time, the dial just a hair off, so there's constant static. And over that static I hear the click-clacking of his computer keys.

A few times, in the middle of the night when I've gotten up for a piss, I can hear him screaming. I know this sounds weird, but he screams softly. He hoarse whisper–yells. That's even worse somehow than if he just let it rip.

I can't make out the words but there they are. Word after word after word. Deep in the phantom hours, when the rest of the world is sleeping, Boaz is lost someplace where he's forgotten he doesn't talk much anymore.

When I knock, he never opens the door. He asks, "What do you need?"

What *I* need. That's a laugh. "Are you okay?"

"Yeah. I'm fine." Three words.

"All right," I say. "Just checking."

Christina Crowley stops by to see him.

She's sitting at the kitchen table, facing Mom, hands around a glass of iced tea. She's more beautiful, more perfect, than I even remembered.

I've just come in from a run. I figure it beats smoking for clearing my head. Turns out I'm not half bad at it.

Sports were Boaz's thing. Soccer. Baseball. He was a pretty decent basketballer for a guy his height. After his games I'd head home with Mom and Abba and watch him go off to a party with his teammates. *Maybe someday*, I'd think.

Today I took a morning run. A Saturday. Wicked hot. The air is thick and apparently it's National Mow Your Lawn Day. I feel like I've inhaled a small patch of grass.

Christina stands up. "Oh my God! Levi! Look at you!"

There's an awkward moment when I think maybe I'm supposed to hug her. One thing I'm pretty sure of is you don't shake hands with a girl. I'm also pretty sure you don't hug a girl with a sweat-soaked T-shirt.

I settle for a wave and busy myself getting water.

"I can't believe how you've grown up." She sits and pulls out the chair next to her. "Come have a seat and tell me what's new with you."

I haven't seen her in three years. That's a pretty decent chunk of my life.

"Not much, really."

"That's not true." Mom wipes the table where I've dripped a bit of sweat. "Levi has started running. And he's finishing up his junior year. And he . . . um . . ." She searches my face. "Come on, baby. Tell Christina about yourself."

I shrug. "I've got Hardwicke for English."

"Oh yeah. I had her too. Does she still have a mustache?"

I remember Christina complaining about Ms. Hardwicke

to Boaz. That's why I mention it. I remember everything about Christina.

"It's pretty much a full-on goatee now."

"Ha." She puts a hand over mine. An electric jolt shoots through my weary body.

Mom clears our empty glasses. She backs her way out of the kitchen with a smile and returns to her laundry.

"I came to see Boaz." Christina leans in close. I can feel her breath on my face. "But I'm getting the message that maybe that's not such a great idea."

God, she's lovely, I think.

Lovely: not a word a guy should ever say out loud, unless he's in the market for a good dope slap, but it sure applies to Christina Crowley.

She's cut her blond hair to just below her chin, revealing the world's most beautiful neck, and she wears no makeup. I hate when girls wear makeup. I mean, you're a girl, right? You've got all this soft skin and eyelashes and stuff. Why would you go and slap paint over those amazing natural resources?

Once I walked in on them in Boaz's bedroom.

If I was sneaking into my brother's room all those times in some sort of attempt to learn about him, or myself, or what might happen to me in four years, I hit the jackpot that rainy December afternoon.

Boaz, tangled in her arms and legs. Their bodies moving slowly. The butterfly tattoo on her left shoulder.

I stood there for longer than I should have. They didn't see me. I backed my way out of the room.

For ages I couldn't look Christina in the eye without my face going hot.

So, now she's here. That's gotta mean something. Maybe he was writing her, calling her, visiting her at Dartmouth, all those times he wasn't writing, calling or visiting us.

I didn't realize how much I've missed looking at her.

"He's not . . ." I'm searching for the right words. "I don't know . . . what you'd call social, I guess."

She takes a deep breath, lets it out slowly, reaches around and grabs the back of that beautiful neck and begins to massage it with her hand.

She was there the night he made his announcement.

Right after he'd finished his salad. It was a regular dinner. A Sunday night with Dov. It was April. The day had been long and lazy. Unseasonably warm. We'd been talking about the shade of pink our neighbors had painted their house. There was nothing about the evening that would have signaled to anybody that this night would become *that night*.

Boaz had been accepted to Cornell, Columbia, Tufts and Berkeley. Everyone was awaiting his decision, Mom with a sort of giddy anticipation that meant she pestered him constantly.

"So?" she asked for the hundredth time. "Anything you'd like to share with the group?"

"Yes, actually." He put down his fork. Pushed back his chair just a little. "I'm joining the Marines. I'll enlist right after graduation."

There was a silence. A pause during which we all considered whether this was some sort of joke. Boaz could be funny.

He wasn't always such a serious person. But it was clear he'd meant what he'd said.

He might as well have said he was going to become a ballerina. That would have come as an equal shock. I know that sounds strange when you consider how our father, our grandfather and even our grandmother were soldiers, but that was Israel. This is America.

"But . . . but . . . that's not what people like us do," Christina said, her lip quivering. When I remember it now, I wonder if maybe it hurt her that he didn't include her in this decision. That he'd gone ahead and made it, and announced it to her along with everyone else.

"What people like us?" Boaz asked.

"People who have other opportunities. Who get into Ivy League schools. Who believe in . . . peace and diplomacy over bullying."

"No, Boaz," Mom said. "No, honey. You aren't thinking clearly. No." Mom's last *no* was tiny. Like she already knew she'd lost.

Abba and Dov said little that night. It was pretty clear where they both stood. Joining up for a war without a clear mission, when it wasn't part of the price of citizenship in the country we all called home, wasn't a choice either of them would have made themselves. And they said this later, each in his own way.

But they didn't fight him the way Mom or Christina did, and I'm not sure Mom has ever been able to forgive Abba for that.

Boaz started to get angry. "This was obviously not an easy

decision, but it's the right one, and it would be nice to know that I've got the support of my family." He looked at Christina. "And my girlfriend."

"But Boaz. Why?" Christina asked. "Why throw away everything you've worked toward?"

"Because I can, I'm able, and I'll be good at it. And if I don't go somebody else will. And because I'm not throwing anything away. I'm doing what's right."

I'd been thinking about him leaving for college. Preparing for it. Wondering what that would mean for me. When you're fourteen, like when you're ten or five or two, you tend to see the world in terms of what everything means for *you*. But I'd only imagined him going to Boston. Or New York. Maybe all the way to northern California.

Not some far-off desert country where he could go and get himself killed.

There were so many things I couldn't wrap my head around.

What would lead somebody like Boaz to give up so much? He had everything, not the least of which was a girl I'd commit a crime for if I thought it might make her glance in my direction.

That night, I was pretty sure he was ready to let her go. But even though Christina was angry, she stuck with him, and they graduated high school as boyfriend and girlfriend, the perfect couple. Whatever happened later, like most of what happened between them, remains a mystery to me.

Nobody bothered to ask what I thought, but I spoke up. My voice was starting to change, and I always cleared my throat before saying anything, not wanting to leave the squeaking to chance.

"Don't do this," I said.

It wasn't so much that I had an opinion about the war, or even any understanding of what Boaz was signing up for. It was more that I couldn't comprehend a distance so far, a change so big, and I was already feeling the change start to happen right then, right there. That night.

"Is he all right?" Christina asks me now.

"I'm not sure."

"Because I don't know if you read the paper, but there are all sorts of horror stories about the way they come home. All these advances we've made in battlefield triage. We keep saving these soldiers with lost limbs or worse, but then we don't know how to take care of them once we get them home."

"No, he's fine. I mean, he hasn't got a scratch on him."

She takes this in. I can see her relief. Then she says, "There's all different sorts of hurt, Levi."

She gives my hand a squeeze and stands up. She kisses the top of my head. "If it seems like a good idea, please tell your brother I stopped by."

She turns to leave.

"Christina."

"Yes?"

All I know is that I don't want her to walk away for good.

"Keep trying, will you?"

"Always."

• • •

Boaz had left her before. For one whole summer, after their junior year in high school. He went to live on Abba's kibbutz in Israel. I went to sleepaway camp. Like Boaz, I'd gone at Abba's insistence, but the only people I left behind were Pearl and Zim, and hard as that might have been for me, you just can't compare Pearl and Zim to Christina.

Boaz didn't want to go, Christina didn't want him to go, but Abba was hell-bent.

"You should know a different way of life," he'd barked.

When I was little, Abba's accent mortified me. Kids around me had trouble understanding what he was saying. They'd look at him funny, with cocked heads and wrinkled noses. And sometimes, they'd laugh at my father. In front of me.

It was more than Abba's accent that shamed me, really, it was the way he sounded sometimes, like he had no soft space inside him. Everything short and sharp. Adjectives were not his friends. Talking to Abba, no matter what the subject, I always had the vague feeling I was getting accused of something.

Abba had become an American in so many ways. He'd married an American woman he met one summer when she was visiting Israel with some college friends. They'd moved together to Boston. Started a family. Raised American sons.

He'd grown comfortable with the easy way in which things came to you in America. But still, every time he opened his mouth, he was the foreigner.

Boaz argued, "But Abba, you left the kibbutz. You didn't want to live there anymore. Why make me go?"

"Because," Abba said, putting a stress on each word like

Boaz didn't have the smarts to understand a simple sentence. "You. Should. Know. A. Different. Way. Of. Life."

They went around and around like that for weeks.

We'd been to Israel twice already, in the psychotic heat of summer. We took the obligatory outings to the Dome of the Rock and the Western Wall. We hiked to the top of Masada and floated in the Dead Sea. But mostly we stayed in a little apartment, drinking lemonade that tasted strange, playing cards with Mom while Abba caught up with old friends in Hebrew.

A different sort of Abba took over on those visits. He bear-hugged men twice his size. Filled the tiny rooms of our apartment with his laughter. He was breathless, suddenly, with more to say than there was time to say it.

I figure Boaz must have been drawn to the adventure in the idea of spending his summer on Abba's kibbutz, because if he really didn't want to go, he would have found some way out of it. Boaz was like that even then. He had convictions you couldn't talk him down from.

Off he went. He loved it, and Abba was pleased. Boaz had gone and learned another way of life. He'd come back tan and lean, more serious, with a Hebrew vocabulary that far surpassed anything either of us ever picked up at Temple Beth Torah.

But he also came back with something else.

Some inkling in him of what he needed to do to become the person he wanted to be, what his responsibilities to the world might involve, and even though this was part of Abba's plan, Boaz took it further than Abba ever imagined.

• • •

"Christina Crowley?" Pearl is finishing my French fries.

"Yep."

"You had serious wood for her the better part of your pre-adolescence!"

Jesus. Was I that obvious?

I'd never said anything to Pearl about Christina. But Pearl is like that. She knows most things, even if she doesn't always come out and say so.

We're sitting in the coffee shop in between our two schools. Sometimes we meet up here, when neither of us feels much like being home. It's a place I go only with Pearl, and the fact that I've never been here with Zim pleases her to no end.

The waitress likes us—the Chinese girl in her schoolgirl uniform and her long-haired boyfriend who's finally starting to grow out of his skinny boy body—and she never seems to mind that we aren't big spenders.

"Don't look all guilt-stricken, Levi," Pearl says. "It's totally normal to lust after your brother's girlfriend. It's textbook, really. And when she's got a pair like Christina Crowley, who could blame you?"

I eat a French fry. It's soggy and cold.

"You know," she says, popping another one in her mouth, "you really shouldn't eat this crap. You need to take better care of your body."

That's a laugh. I'm running the equivalent of a marathon a week. Pearl still smokes. *And* she's eating more than her share of my fries.

"So did Boaz come out of his lair to see her?"

I just look at her: *What do you think?*

"Right. Of course not." She stirs some fake sweetener into her coffee and sighs. We sit like that. In silence awhile, but not an uncomfortable silence like the kind at my dinner table. There's no such thing as uncomfortable when it comes to Pearl.

She leans in closer. "So what was it like to see Christina again?"

I look at her, just like before.

"Right," she says, nodding her head, and then she walks me home, her arm linked through mine.

When I hand in my chemistry take-home final, Mr. Hopper shakes my hand with meaning. He tries to catch my darting eyes. I brush the hair off my forehead. Try staring back.

Maybe if I look him in the eye, I think, *he'll decide he doesn't need to say anything. Maybe if I look him in the eye he'll decide to bump up my grade.*

"He's a hero, Levi," Mr. Hopper finally says. "I hope you're proud."

He doesn't leave his fucking room, Mr. Hopper.

"Of course I'm proud," I say. "We all are."

This sort of thing keeps happening to me. And it's not just the teachers.

Sophie Olsen crashes our do-nut power breakfast in the courtyard before the first bell. Zim's a bit of a scammer, and he's taken to selling packages of do-nuts in the courtyard at a 100 percent markup, so when Sophie comes up I figure she needs a morning sugar rush.

"Hi, fellas," she says.

Zim just stands there with do-nut-filled cheeks, like some sort of deranged chipmunk. He holds out a pack of do-nuts. She looks at it like he's offering her someone's severed hand.

"Hi, Sophie," I say.

"How are things going?" she asks.

"Okay, I guess."

She takes her hand and puts it on my forearm. "Really?"

It's funny the way a face as pretty as hers can take on the same exact look as the face of a pockmarked old man like Mr. Hopper.

"Really."

"Okay, then." She strokes my arm a little. "See you around."

Zim finally swallows his do-nut. "What's wrong with you?"

"What?"

"She's practically *begging* you to ask her out."

"I don't think so." And anyway, there's seriously limber, silky-haired Rebecca Walsh, otherwise known as Dylan Fredricks's girlfriend. There's Christina Crowley.

I don't say this last part out loud. Zim would have a total conniption if he thought I was blowing off Sophie Olsen because of my obsession with two girls I'm as likely to date as I am to win the Pillsbury Bake-Off.

Anyway, if not a date with Sophie Olsen, I *am* hoping this bizarre attention might help me get the job at Videorama. Everyone wants the job at Videorama. I'm not used to getting whatever it is everyone else wants, but I figure if I ever had the chance, now is it.

Problem is, Zim wants it too. I don't feel so bad about using my status as Brother of Returning Soldier to bump another worthy soul out of line, unless that worthy soul is one of my two best friends.

Bob, the store manager, used to rent movies to Boaz and Christina. They'd bring home three, sometimes four DVDs and spend their Saturday nights under blankets on the couch.

"When's your brother going to stop by?" he asked when I went to drop off my application.

"I don't know. Sometime soon."

"Well, you tell him this from me, you hear: Bob at Video-rama says he's a hero."

"Sure thing, Bob."

He slid my application to the top of his stack.

So, I'm thinking about all this after leaving Zim in the courtyard—the new ways people are looking at and talking to me—when I pass Eddie Taylor in the hall.

We were pretty decent friends in elementary school and I've forgotten why that isn't the case anymore. Probably there's no reason other than that this kind of thing happens when you're younger. One day you're friends with someone and the next day you're not. It's kind of a bitch, but what can you do? Anyway, Eddie's an okay guy. He's smart. And perpetually good-natured, which I figure we'd all be if we smoked as much dope as Eddie.

He's all student activisty. You know the type: bumper stickers on his car, buttons on his jacket and political slogans on his worn-out T-shirts. He spearheaded the antiwar rally held on a Saturday afternoon last fall that drew more students than when the varsity soccer team played the finals.

"Hey." He wheels around. We were just about to pass each other without saying a word, which we do every day. "Nice shirt," he says.

I look down at my chest. I'm wearing a T-shirt with a picture of John Lennon in round-framed sunglasses. "Thanks, man."

Eddie continues moving toward his first class, then flips back around again. "Listen, I'm really glad your brother made it home safe."

This time it catches me totally off guard.

On the one hand, I want to say something about how just because my brother chose to enter this war doesn't mean I'm for it, and that if the circumstances of my life were different, I might have shown up at the antiwar rally last fall.

I want to say that.

But I also want to say something about this protest Eddie organized. Something about people who sit around all day getting high, and then have the nerve to complain about the people who put their own lives at risk every time they swing their feet out of bed and drop them on the floor.

I want to say both of these things, and I'd settle for either, but I say, "Thanks, Eddie." And I continue down the path to first period.

See, I never got any sort of a chance to make up my own mind about this war.

I've just become a character, we all have, in a story we don't get to write ourselves.

· · ·

Pearl stops by for a study session. I've got a Spanish final coming up. She's got comparative religion. Pearl gets bored as soon as we crack our books, so she starts digging through my closet. She changes into an old pair of my jeans that fit her snugly.

"Ooooh. Skinny jeans!" she says as she checks herself out in the mirror.

We flee to the roof.

Pearl is now officially dating the guy who sells popcorn at the movie theater. He's her fifth boyfriend.

Girlfriends I've had: zero.

I haven't even had the Maddie Green kind of non-girlfriend like Zim. I've had my share of drunken, fumbly, grabby party moments. But who hasn't?

"I think you'll like Popcorn Guy," Pearl says.

"I doubt it."

"Yeah, you're probably right. He's not really your type."

I pick up a broken piece of the roof's slate tile and hurl it into the yard.

Pearl lies back and closes her eyes to the sun.

"Levi, what's going on?"

"What do you mean?"

"You know what I mean. With Boaz. And with everyone. It doesn't seem like much has changed around here since he's come back."

"That's because he's not really back. He just hangs out in his room and comes downstairs occasionally to eat. He's the surly teenager he never was when he was a real teenager."

"What do you think he's up to in there?"

"I have no idea."

"I hate to sound like an after-school special, but do you think maybe it's drugs?"

That question has crossed my mind. You hear about soldiers coming back so screwed up they turn into drug addicts. That idea is totally at odds with what I know about Boaz, but at this point, I can't rule anything out.

"Maybe he has an online girlfriend," Pearl says. She stubs out her cigarette on the sole of her hot-pink Puma. "Or maybe he's stuck in a bidding war on eBay."

There's a knock at the door.

"Come in," I shout.

I'm expecting Zim, or maybe Mom with a pile of laundry. When the door opens there stands Boaz, looking like he's gone and gotten himself lost.

"Hey!" I scramble back in through my window.

"Hi, Boaz!" It comes out like a squawk. Pearl can't do peppy.

"Hey, Pearl."

She starts shoving her books into her backpack.

"Well, boys, I gotta run. Mama Goldblatt no likey when Pearl's late for dinner."

She darts around Bo and turns to shoot me the *call me or I'll kill you* look.

"It's broken," Bo says.

"What's broken?"

"My computer."

I think of pointing out that my days as a card-carrying

member of the computer club are over. But still. Here's my brother. Standing in my room. And he's talking.

I don't want to ruin the moment.

Plus there's no denying I know a thing or two about computers. I'm just not sure what I can do about Boaz's. It's ancient. The same big, bulky desktop he used in high school. It's a small miracle it's held up this long.

"Do you want me to come take a look?"

"You don't mind?"

"Not at all."

I follow him down the hall to his room.

This is it. My invitation into the den of darkness.

It's a colossal mess.

I mean epic.

A bare mattress off its frame lies on the floor with nothing but a tangled cloud sheet. Clothes, shoes, towels all over the floor. A couple of barbells, and papers everywhere. All the while the radio spits out static.

Mom would have a coronary if he ever let her in here.

I try my best to read all this as a good sign. Maybe he's letting loose. Rebelling against the rigid life of a marine.

And anyway, messiness is something I can understand.

I make straight for the computer. I don't want Boaz to think I'm inspecting or judging his room, even though that's what I'm doing.

His computer screen has gone pale gray, and in its center is a sad little face with Xs for eyes and a tongue sticking out an upside-down U of a mouth.

The message indisputable: Game Over.

I drum my fingers on the desk. "I'm afraid it's your mother-board."

"What's that?"

"You know, the central system that makes your computer work properly."

"That's bad, right?"

"It's not good."

"Shit." He sits down in his chair and puts his face in his hands.

Maybe I should comfort him. Say something encouraging. But instead I use this moment, with Boaz's eyes in a web of his fingers, to take a closer look around the room.

The papers on the floor. They're maps. All of them.

Some are printed from the computer. Some look like the kind you'd buy at your local gas station if you ever left the house. Above his bed is an old Rand McNally map of the United States that once hung in my room. Abba bought it for me when I first started trying to understand places in relationship to each other, pestering him with my endless questions: *Where's Boston? Where's Israel? Where's Gotham City?*

I wonder where Boaz found it. It's been a lifetime since I saw it last.

I squint at the pastel-colored states and baby-blue oceans and notice that the right side, the Atlantic, is covered in pencil scrawlings, but I'm too far away to make any sense out of them.

Boaz lets out a deep, guttural groan. "Damn it," he whispers. For a second, I think he might actually cry.

Suddenly, I can see him at nine, running into the house

with a wrist bent the wrong way. He'd taken a fall off his skateboard and was screaming and cursing, running around in circles, but his eyes were dry as the desert.

I've never seen my brother in tears. Watching him cry over a dead computer is something I just don't think I can handle.

"It's all right," I whisper. I almost place my hand on his shoulder. "It's probably time you get a new one anyway."

"Shitshitshitshitshitshit."

I picture a trip to the Apple Store. A swarm of tattooed hipsters in matching black T-shirts and headsets asking Boaz how they could help him. I know I can't watch him go through that.

"Look, I can get it for you if you want. Or you could just use my laptop. I've got finals to study for and I don't need it all that much. As long as I can have it for a few hours in the afternoon to check my e-mail and visit my favorite porn sites, I'm all set."

This doesn't earn even the hint of a grin.

I decide to give it one more go. "Right now I'm all about Gigantic Jiggling Jugs dot com."

Nothing.

Boaz clears his throat. "Can I print?"

"Of course. I'll configure it. No problem."

He lifts his head. Cloudy eyes and an unreadable face.

"Thanks, little brother," he says.

Even though it might seem like I had this in mind when I offered my computer to him, I really didn't. I promise. I'd swear on my grandmother's grave if she hadn't bucked tradition and insisted on a burial at sea.

I didn't plan this.

But sometimes you're handed an opportunity.

And every day, when I get home from school, Boaz meets me at the threshold to his room, and he puts that opportunity right into my hands.

My days of hunting for some trace of Boaz, running my fingertips over his possessions may be long gone, but there are other ways to retrieve information.

I know I shouldn't.

I can't tell what my brother is thinking or what is happening to him inside his messy room, but I can find out where he's been.

Virtualsoldier.com

Memorialspace.net

Inthelineofduty.com

Desertcam.net

And a long array of sites with detailed maps of the northeastern United States from Boston to the Chesapeake Bay.

He has an e-mail account, and I know I could figure out how to log in as Boaz, but that, for the time being at least, is a line I can't cross.

Maybe I do believe in something after all.

FOUR

ABBA WAKES ME at eight-thirty.

Eight-thirty on a Sunday? To make matters worse, I was having a dream about Christina Crowley. All oil-slick slippery with no shred of a plot. The butterfly on her shoulder. Things were just getting good when: "Levi! *Kum!* It's time we get to that fence!"

Now it's nearly two in the afternoon, and I'm covered with sawdust, nowhere near done with the fence and out of things to talk about with Abba. The obvious topic for discussion is why *I'm* out here instead of *Boaz*, when we all know that he's the one who knows how to fix things. He knows how to work with tools that rattle your limbs and blow out your eardrums. But I just let the electric sander eat up the silences.

Zim stops by, hoping I'll go shoot some baskets, which typically involves me sitting down watching him shoot baskets, because any other way is just downright humiliating.

He beats a quick retreat before Abba enlists him in Project Fence.

A big storm last winter knocked a branch off our neighbors'

tree, which knocked down our fence, which to my sense of order means the neighbors should be the ones out here fixing it, but Abba says their mess is our mess too.

I hand him a freshly sanded board. He inspects it. Slides his big hands up and down the flat sides. He blows some dust off its edges and nods his approval. I hold it upright while Abba fills a hole in the ground with wet cement. I watch beads of sweat congregate around his bald spot.

He sticks a post into the hole. He holds it there and I watch him count to thirty under his breath.

Abba could have lived his life like this. Instead of running Reuben Katznelson Insurance with five branches in the greater Boston area, he could have stayed on the kibbutz and spent his days fixing fences. Picking oranges. Maybe milking cows.

But he wanted to own his own house. He wanted to eat at his own dining table, line his own pockets with his own hard-earned money and raise his children in a melting pot. In the land of opportunity. In a country that wasn't constantly defending its very right to exist.

When we finish, Abba strips down and showers himself with the garden hose. I take in the stomach that's now more flab than muscle. His pale and beefy back. The mole or two on his ass.

I'm pretty sure there's nothing in the world uglier than the sight of your own father's pubic hair.

"B'seder, Levi. Go inside and get me a towel."

For Abba, the immigrant, everything was turning out just fine for a while.

He had the house and the dining table and the pockets. He had the American wife he'd met in Israel who would have stayed on happily but returned because it was what *he* wanted.

He had the American sons.

Then Boaz had to go and make his choice.

And now I'm out here on a Sunday fixing fences.

I dream of maps.

Continents and oceans. States. Highways. Rivers. Places I've never been swarm beneath my closed eyelids.

Maps. Maps. Everywhere maps.

I'm desperate to understand his maps, but I don't have the courage to ask, and anyway, Boaz doesn't give me the chance.

Why? I want to ask him. *Why all those maps? What are you planning? Where are you going? Or are you just dreaming, like I am, of someplace else?*

We're sitting at dinner with Dov when it strikes me.

"I've been thinking about it," I say. "And I think, maybe, I want to go to Oberlin."

Dov looks at Abba. "What's this nice lady talking about?"

"Oberlin. It's a college, Dov. Hard to believe, but Levi's almost a senior. He's got to start looking at colleges."

Abba says this like it's just occurred to him. By the time Boaz was taking final exams his junior year, Abba had a three-sheet list of schools on yellow legal paper.

Mom wipes her mouth with her napkin. "That's wonderful news, baby. It's a great school. I have a friend who went there and she loved it."

"Where's Oberlin?" Dov asks.

Aha.

See, Dov's a smart man. He knows a ton. But everyone has a weakness, even Dov, and his is the geography of the United States. It's probably because when my grandmother died Dov moved from the kibbutz straight to Boston and has barely been anyplace since.

I put down my fork. "It's in Ohio."

"So that would be west of here."

Abba laughs. "It certainly isn't east, Dov."

"Shut up, smart-ass."

"We have a map somewhere, right?" I say. "I'll show him."

"We must. Somewhere." Abba shrugs and goes back to frowning at his eggplant.

"What about that Rand McNally map that used to be in my room?"

At this Bo turns his gaze on me, laserlike. I can feel heat.

Mom says, "Why don't you show Dov on your computer. Find a map online. That way you can show him the school's Web site too."

"Ohio." Dov shakes his head. "Who ever heard of such a place?"

Pearl broke up with Popcorn Guy. If he had another name, I never learned it.

"He just wasn't the kind of boy I could bring home to Mama Goldblatt."

"Your mom doesn't even know you date."

We're driving around without any place to go. Zim is stretched out across the backseat. It's Saturday night.

"And he misused the word *penultimate*. He told me that *Asteroids of Doom* was the penultimate popcorn movie."

"He *is* Popcorn Guy, after all," Zim says. "This *is* his area of expertise."

I point to the left. Pearl turns.

"So that's why you broke up with him? Because he doesn't know what *penultimate* means?" That sounds awfully short-sighted to me.

"Tell me what *penultimate* means, Levi." She throws a look over her shoulder at Zim. "I'm not asking you, Richard Zimmerman, because everyone knows you're a moron."

"You won't get any argument from me," Zim replies.

"Are you testing me?" I ask.

"Yes."

"*Penultimate* means second to last."

"See?" She slaps my thigh. "If you weren't so homely I'd totally date you."

I point to the right. She turns again.

"Where are we going, anyway?"

"I don't know. We could go get milk shakes?"

"Screw you, Levi." She shoves me hard.

"Ow. What?"

"Have you even looked at me lately? I'm so fucking fat! What normal Chinese girl gets fat like this? I'm supposed to be delicate. Diminutive. Demure."

"You're insane."

"I blame the Jews. Mama Goldblatt and her goddamn brisket. It's not natural. Biologically speaking, I should be on a totally different kind of diet."

Zim sits up and leans forward. "So let's go get egg rolls."

"No." She makes a turn onto Route 2 heading west. "Let's go to the pond."

We park underneath a cluster of pines.

The dried-out needles crunch beneath my flip-flops.

"Let's walk," Pearl says.

The loop around the pond is a little over a mile. She starts out ahead and Zim and I jog to catch up. The moon is full. Its reflection spiderwebs its way across the water. A warm wind rustles the leaves. Laughter rolls in from far off in the woods. I'm with my two best friends in the world and it's a night so beautiful it's like it sprang from the pages of a child's picture book. It's the kind of night that might fill another person with a sense of peace, but for me, all a night like this does is shine a light on the places where everything is going wrong.

Pearl is panting.

"You know," I say, "you really should quit smoking."

"Stuff it, Saint Levi."

We walk without talking. Somehow Zim and Pearl sense that I'm not up for it.

A boulder appears on the path in front of us. Pearl and Zim take to one side and I take to the other. I almost whisper *Bread and butter*, but only because I've heard Mom say it a thousand times, not because superstitions carry any weight with me at all.

"It used to be only me he ignored," I finally say, "but now he's ignoring the world."

Pearl slows her pace so she's walking by my side. "If it makes you feel any better, he used to ignore me too."

"Not me," Zim says. "He was always really cool to me. And don't hate me for saying this, Levi, but he was pretty cool to you too. He just had a lot of stuff going on at the end of high school, and he had to deal with your parents, and how everyone freaked out about his decision, and I'm not sure it's fair to take all that so personally."

I stop in my tracks. I feel Pearl's hand on my wrist.

I don't know if she's trying to hold me back from punching Zim, or if she's just trying to show me she's on my side.

Pearl lets go and it feels like she's uncorked me, like all the blood drains right out of my body. I'm not going to punch Zim. Of course I'm not going to punch Zim. I'm not filled with fight.

I'm filled with worry.

"It's just . . . I don't know. I don't know what's happening with him. He doesn't do anything. He just spends all his time on the Internet," I say.

"You've just described the entire American population under the age of forty-five," Pearl says.

"And he looks at maps. Lots and lots of maps. I guess this could be taken as a good sign, like he's actually interested in something, but it sure doesn't feel like it."

"What kind of Web sites does he go to?" Zim asks.

"How would I know?"

"Because you check his history when you take back your laptop."

"I do?"

"Yeah, dude. You do."

"Yeah. I do."

"So?"

I let out a big sigh. "It's bleak."

We've arrived back at the parking lot.

It's almost midnight. I'd be worried about getting home if I had a curfew or if I thought anyone was waiting up for me.

"How bleak?" Zim and Pearl ask in unison. They look at each other and, because they're so rarely in synch, they can't help but smile a little.

I tell them how he spends his days looking at desert combat video shot by the shaky hands of soldiers with their pocket-sized cameras. How he visits Web pages that have outlived their subjects, turned from sites where cocky young guys with names like Spike once blogged about scratchy army toilet paper into online memorials. Virtual warehouses storing the grief of others.

I tell them something they already know. That Boaz used to be one of those people who had everything. But still, there were things he wanted. Things to fight for. Even if that part of him cost us all so much.

I tell them how he's gone and disappeared.

Pearl stops with the keys in her hand and looks at me over the roof of her car. Her face stone straight. Very un-Pearl-like.

"He's in there somewhere, Levi. Really, he is, and he'll be back. Somehow he'll be back."

Zim nods his head.

I want to believe them. And I try.

But the moon is gone now, vanished behind some clouds, taking the warm air with it, and this is no longer a night that might bring somebody peace.

It's a night full of worry.

And for me that worry is this: maybe he *is* back. Maybe this is it.

There's a saying about the military that you go in a boy and come back a man. But I'm pretty sure Boaz went in a man and came back a ghost.

FIVE

When I was little I used to sleep with my parents. I'd wake up, find my way down the darkened hallway and invent some sort of excuse for why I'd arrive at their bedside in the dead of night.

My foot aches. There's a noise outside my window. There's something itchy in my sheets.

I don't sleep with my parents anymore because, well, that would be totally gross. But I'm still someone who wakes, for no real reason, in the middle of almost every single night.

Now when I do, more often than not, I hear Boaz. Sometimes it's typing. Tonight, I hear him soft-screaming.

I don't get up. I don't go to his door or go see if there's anything I can do to help him through the dark hours.

I reach for my radio alarm clock and I fill the room with music from my favorite station. A song I've never heard.

Tonight I turn the dial. Just a touch. A fraction of a fraction too small to measure, until I can no longer hear my brother.

All I can hear is static.

● ● ●

I see Christina when I go with Pearl to a movie at a different theater from the one where Popcorn Guy works. She sits three rows ahead of us. Her date is tall, thin. Long, tanned arms. Blond goatee. A T-shirt from Boston College Law School.

At some point during the first half of the movie he leans over and whispers into her hair. He kisses the arch of her neck. She lowers her head onto his shoulder.

I grab Pearl and try rushing her out the door at the start of the final credits, before the houselights come up.

"I gotta pee," she says.

"C'mon, Pearl. Can't we just get out of here?"

"Did you see the size of my soda? Sorry." She shrugs, her hands comically covering her crotch. She darts into the bathroom.

I step outside and study the posters for the movies coming soon to a theater near me. I wonder when the ticket-buying world will finally tire of movies spoofing fringe sports.

"Levi!"

I could pretend it's not my name. Bill. Bill would work for me right about now. Bill, the guy who just can't wait for the next movie about an Ultimate Frisbee team down on its luck.

She comes and stands beside me.

"Hi, Christina."

She holds out a packet of Twizzlers. "Want one?"

I don't, but I take one anyway. Her date seems to have disappeared. Maybe he has a girl's bladder like Pearl.

"How are things?"

"By *things* do you mean Boaz?"

It comes out sounding a lot pissier than I intend it to. She takes a step back and looks into the Twizzler packet as if she might find something valuable in there.

"Yes. I do."

"Well, if you really want to know, he never leaves his room, and he barely talks, and he spends all his time online, and sometimes I wake up to the sound of him screaming."

She sighs. She reaches over and she takes my hand. She must still think I'm a small child. She was always kind to me this way. She showed me the sort of affection a sister might to a much younger brother.

But now it's just sort of awkward.

Yet not so awkward that I let go, because it's not so often, in fact it's never, that I get to hold the hand of a girl like Christina.

"How about Reuben and Amanda?"

"You know my parents," I say, but then I realize she doesn't. She knows who they were before Boaz left. And that's a whole lot different from who they are now. She knew them when Abba used to make Mom laugh. When Mom used to paint. When they'd listen to music together even though they have such different tastes, and sometimes, they'd dance in the living room and I'd cover my eyes because it was too embarrassing to watch. She knew them when there was a whole world we might talk about at the dinner table and nothing was off-limits, not politics, not war.

"What can I do?" she asks. "Really, I'll do anything."

Mr. Blond Goatee returns. So does Pearl. They're standing next to each other, a few feet away, staring at us. He's probably thinking: *Why is this kid holding my girlfriend's hand?*

And Pearl is probably thinking: *He should have gone for the boob.*

"I don't know. You could stop by again? Get him outside? Maybe take him for a drive. Get him out of the house and into the fresh air. Talk to him."

"I'll give it a try. I'm probably not his favorite person in the world, so I can't promise I'll get anywhere, but I'll give it a try."

She untangles her fingers from mine, but I can feel her hand, the warmth and softness of it, long after she wanders off under the arm of her boyfriend.

I go to see Dov.

I don't call ahead. I figure my chances of finding Dov at home are pretty good. He never seems to do much beyond visiting us and loitering at the Armenian deli.

I arrive at the building just as someone is leaving. I slip in the front door and walk up two flights of stairs to apartment G.

I hear his voice from across the room.

"Hold your horses! I'm coming! Just a minute!"

Dov sounds harassed even though I only rang the buzzer once.

"What, what?" he's saying, but then he slaps on a broad smile when he sees that it's me. "Oh, look. The Avon Lady came calling."

"Hi, Dov."

He kisses my cheek. "Come in, come in. Can I get you a coffee? A soda? A shot of whiskey?"

"I'm good."

Dov's kitchen, living room and dining room are all part of the same square space. He has a worn-out plaid couch and a TV. A round table with two mismatched folding chairs. His bedroom is dark. The window looks out onto the brick wall of the building next door. He sleeps on a single mattress.

It's the apartment of someone who long ago threw in the towel.

"To what do I owe this pleasure?" He pats a spot on the couch next to him.

I sit. Dov puts a hand on my knee.

"I don't know."

There's a picture of my grandmother in a frame on Dov's nearly empty bookshelf. Dov doesn't keep books. He buys them used from the library and donates them back.

The photo is black-and-white. She's sitting on the beach under an umbrella, her hair tied back in a checkered scarf, caught mid-laugh. I wonder what that laugh sounded like. How she smelled. If she had soft skin.

After she died, Dov left the kibbutz and moved to Boston to be near their only son. I was born six months later.

We sit side by side on the couch without speaking. Somebody is screaming at somebody else in an apartment upstairs. A dog barks feebly from the courtyard below.

Dov must have some idea of why I'm here. He's not totally

clueless. But Dov just sits. The picture of patience. A man who has nothing but time.

I take a deep breath and let it out. "I'm worried about Boaz."

"Oh, *motek*. Of course you are," Dov says. And then, "We all are."

"So why isn't anybody doing anything?" My shirt is sticking to my back. I had to walk fourteen blocks from the nearest T stop.

"Maybe I'll take that soda now," I say.

Dov shoots up from the couch, happy to have a task. He roots around in his cupboards and then pours a generic brand of cola into a jelly jar with ice.

"Listen, Levi." He sits back down next to me. "We all have our ways of dealing with the shit life serves up. The terrible things we've seen. The pain of loss. Change. Whatever." He turns my chin to face him. He tucks a strand of hair behind my ear. "We have to let him go through what he needs to go through. We can't expect too much too soon. It's not what we hope for, but it's to be expected. We just have to wait."

"Dov," I say, and I feel my cheeks redden, "I'm tired of waiting."

There's a danger in what I've just said. Or at least in the way it sounded. I'm keenly aware from growing up around Dov and Abba that self-indulgence isn't something to be tolerated. It's a singularly American phenomenon, Dov and Abba believe—the child who thinks the world revolves around him.

It's not really what I mean, though. This time, for a change,

I'm not really talking about myself. And maybe Dov gets that, because he doesn't scold. Instead he says, "I know, *motek*. It isn't fair."

"I know about waiting. It does nothing. No good at all. But it's all anyone's doing."

Dov looks at me carefully.

"Your parents, you know. They do their best. They're trying to give him the space he needs."

"I guess so. But . . . I think there's something else."

"What?"

"I don't know. It's just . . . I think he's up to something. He's planning something. He's going somewhere, and I don't know why, or where, or what he's going to do, but it doesn't feel right. None of this feels right."

I sit in the sticky silent company of my grandfather. Waiting.

"There are ~~~~~~~~~ gs we can look into if it gets to~~~ ~~~~~~~ with your parents. But we're n~~~~ ~~~~~~~ before his release, and he's been ~~~~~~~~~~ at least, we need to give that ~~~~

"Okay."

Dov puts ~~~~~~~ the back of my neck. He grabs my hair with his ~~~~ and gives it a tug.

"You're a good boy, Levi," he says. "A good, good boy."

Just like she promised, Christina stops by. It's a Saturday afternoon. Mom and Abba are off at a movie. It's the thing they still do together, go to the movies. It doesn't matter the topic, the style, the genre—for them, each and every movie is an escape.

I'm sitting on the steps when Christina arrives, watching Zim's little brother mow my lawn. It used to be my job, but I guess Mom got sick of nagging me. Then Mini Chubby Zim, who gets his entrepreneurial streak from his older brother, went and started a neighborhood lawn-mowing business. Not that I want him out of a job, and God knows the kid needs the exercise, but as I sit here I think, *No more.*

From this day on, I mow my own lawn.

Christina checks her reflection in her rearview mirror before stepping out of the car. She's wearing a tank top and cut-off jean shorts that highlight the miraculous length of her legs. In her bare feet she still stands a good inch taller than me.

She sits down and pushes up her sunglasses. I've never been so close to that butterfly in all my life and it takes super-human strength not to reach out and touch it.

"For the record, his name is Max," she says. "And he's really very nice."

"Who?"

"My boyfriend."

"Oh. Him."

She takes a long sip from the iced coffee she brought with her.

"You know, when Boaz and I were together . . . that was years ago. I mean, so much has—"

"You don't need to tell me this," I say, even though I've more or less demanded she explain herself by acting like her jilted lover. Jesus, I'm pathetic.

"I know. It's just that—"

"Look," I say. "I'm just glad you're here."

We sit like this on the steps for a while, long after the lawn is done.

"So? How should we do this?" she finally asks.

"I hadn't planned that far ahead."

"Should I go up to his room?"

I think about the stale air. The mattress on the floor. The tangle of clothes and sheets. The maps everywhere.

I think about that day I walked in on them.

"No, let me. You stay here."

It's cool inside the house. Quiet. My eyes take time adjusting from the brightness of the day. I put the pads of my fingers to Boaz's door. I scratch lightly with what's left of my compulsively bitten nails.

"Boaz?"

"Yeah?"

"Can I come in?"

"Hold on."

He comes to the door. He cracks it open and then fills up the space.

"What's up?"

"Christina Crowley is here to see you."

I don't know why I use her last name. Like there could ever be another Christina.

"I know," he says.

"You do?"

He gestures over his shoulder. "I saw her car."

That he bothers to pull up the shade and look out his

window strikes me as a gigantic leap in the right direction. Funny how quickly the little things become the big things.

"She'd like to see you."

Boaz shifts uncomfortably. He moves something from one hand to the other and then holds it behind his back. A shoe box. I recognize it immediately. The black and red top and the picture of a clown in comically large shoes. It's a box from Marty Muldoon's. They used to give out Tootsie Pops with your sneakers and they went out of business around the time I grew too old to shop there anymore.

Boaz used to keep that box in the back of his closet. Inside he put everything too special to sit unprotected on his shelf. The kinds of things he didn't want anybody, mainly me, to touch.

I have to admit, I looked for that box once Boaz left home, but like so much else, it had gone missing.

"She's out on the front steps," I say. "Waiting. I'm going to my room."

Five minutes pass before I hear Bo's door open. I hear him on the stairs. I hear the creaking of the screen door and then I hear it close again. I wait for the sound of Christina's car starting up, the sound of my brother finally going somewhere, but that sound never comes.

He's only gone about half an hour, and when he comes back he goes straight to his cave. I hustle down the stairs and catch Christina just as she's about to pull away from the curb. Boaz's window looks out to the front, and now that I know he actually lifts his shade, I feel the need to make this quick.

"So?"

I can see that she's been crying. Puffy eyes and splotched cheeks. She wipes her face with the hem of her tank top and in the process I catch the briefest glimpse of her bare stomach.

It strikes me now that seeing each other again couldn't possibly have been easy for either of them. I have nothing, no point of reference. No way to know how that must feel.

"Well, thanks," I offer.

I also, clearly, have no understanding of how to talk to girls who've been crying.

"For what?"

"For getting him out of the house."

"We went for a walk," she says. "He wouldn't get in the car. I wanted to take him to this place we used to go, this spot in the woods near the pond, but he refused to get in my car. I asked if he still had something against my driving. He used to be the worst backseat driver. Always criticizing. But no, he said he wouldn't get in anyone's car. No car at all."

"Okay . . ." I have no idea what else to say.

All I know is I want to reach out and stroke her cheek, to erase the redness, the puffiness, the sadness.

"So I said, *Well, if you don't ride around in cars anymore, how'd you even get home from the airport?*" She readjusts the mirror.

Then she turns to me. "He said he walked."

I remember the night Boaz came home. How he just appeared at the door. Suddenly. Silently.

"He needs help, Levi. Beyond what you, or your family, or certainly I can give him. You all must know that."

"He's been deemed healthy."

I can't believe I say this. It sounded so lame when Dov said it to me and it sounds even lamer now.

"What does that mean?"

"I'm not really sure." I look up to Boaz's window. I can't tell for the glare of the sun if the shade is up or down. "You'd better go."

I straighten up and put my hand on the roof of her car. I give it a slap and she takes this as a cue to drive away without looking back.

SIX

I GET THE JOB AT VIDEORAMA and I break the news to Zim while watching him shoot baskets.

He takes it pretty well.

"That's okay, man," he says. "I'm still waiting to hear from the hair salon. I think my chances there are excellent."

The thing is, he's not kidding. He's not going to cut hair or anything, he's just going to sweep it up off the floor, but he's hoping if he proves himself, he may get the chance to wash it from time to time.

"All that lady hair," he says wistfully. "So totally awesome." In case you hadn't already figured it out, Zim is kind of a freak.

Pearl got a job at Frozurt, this frozen yogurt place three blocks from Videorama.

Finals are almost over. Then there'll be a whole round of parties I'm likely to get invited to now that I'm a minor celebrity at school.

I've been waiting for news of standardized test scores or a winning baseball team or some sort of PTA meeting to bump the following words, built out of magnetized black block letters, from the big white sign in front of the main entrance to the school:

WELCOME HOME, BAY STATE HIGH GRADUATE
BOAZ KATZNELSON, AMERICAN HERO

It's been up there ten days now. Like Bowers's little morning assembly speech wasn't enough.

Suddenly I've become the guy everyone goes out of his way to slap on the back, or say hello to, or share information with about the big party after finals that might have otherwise been kept a secret from someone with my social standing. The whole situation just sort of creeps me out. I want those letters gone, but it doesn't much matter what I want.

I guess I understand why they'd put that up. Bay State doesn't have much of a history of graduating eighteen-year-old marines. Most seniors go on to top colleges or at least low-tier colleges for spoiled rich kids.

So the school is taking some sort of pride in him, and I get that, I do. But they don't know what all this has done to him.

I don't mention the sign to anyone at home, but now Mom is dropping me off at school because she needs the car I usually drive. Zim is out sick with some totally manufactured ailment, so I can't catch a ride with him, which means that on top of suffering the indignity of being dropped off at school by my mother, I'm staring down the dark tunnel of a do-nutless morning.

"Why didn't you tell me about this?" She puts the car in park and gazes at the sign. "It's wonderful, don't you think?"

"I don't know, Mom. I guess so."

"Well, I'm going inside to tell Judy how much we all appreciate this."

Judy Ulene is the principal. Only parents are allowed to call her Judy.

"I'm guessing you haven't told her yourself."

"No, Mom, I haven't."

"Why not?"

I know I'm getting accused of something here, but I'm not totally certain of what. Laziness? Thoughtlessness? Self-absorption?

Any of these is way better than what I've got a feeling she's really digging into me for: not supporting my brother enough.

"Because," I say. "I guess I don't think that a sign is all that important."

The bell has already rung for first period and we're parked in the loading zone. Some stragglers are racing full speed up the steps to the school, but time has slowed down inside this car.

In some ways, we're on the brink of having one of the first real conversations we've had in years.

"Care to explain?"

"Mom. Those words up there . . . they're just empty words, put up by some underpaid janitor on a shaky ladder."

"That is your brother." Spit flies from her mouth and hits the windshield.

"No, Mom. My brother is home holed up in his room. He won't do anything. Or say anything. Or go anywhere. He won't ride in a car. Did you know that? He doesn't need to be worshipped by people who don't know him or understand him. He needs help."

Mom slumps down into her seat, and I start to feel bad for snatching this small moment of happiness from her.

"What he needs is time," she says. "Time to readjust. To remember who he was and what he wants his life to be. He needs us. To be with his family again." Her voice has lost most of its size.

"Don't you think maybe what he needs is some psychiatric help?"

"They screen all returning soldiers for mental health issues before they're discharged. He passed. They said he's healthy."

"So I've heard."

"Look, he's fine. He's going to be fine. He has us. He has our undying love and support. He just needs time."

Mom turns to me, all optimism suddenly.

I can't quite figure her out. I mean, she's a really smart woman. She grew up with really smart parents. There's no reason for such a blind spot when it comes to Boaz, except that I guess she's always had a blind spot when it comes to Boaz. He can do no wrong. Nothing can go wrong.

She's wearing the smile I've grown accustomed to. The kind that it takes some effort to believe in.

"I'm going in there to thank Judy. And you, young man"—she reaches over and tousles my hair—"are going to go ask your teacher's forgiveness for arriving so terribly late to class."

I run almost every day now, and when I do, I chant these words to myself: *It's a marathon, not a sprint. It's a marathon, not a sprint.*

I can go farther, longer, harder when I don't focus on the distance between the place where my aching legs strike the potholed pavement and the place where I can finally slow to a walk, stretch my arms over my head and catch my breath.

It's a marathon, not a sprint.

Then it strikes me today, when I'm not even thinking about it, 'cause that's how I find most things strike me, that it's the same slogan used to justify why we've been in this war so long, why so many lives have been lost, why so many soldiers have come home without arms or legs or traces of their former selves.

It's a marathon, not a sprint.

It's the same idea too. Don't worry about the finish line. Don't question what you're doing. Just quiet your mind and keep up the pace.

"What we need," Dov says, "is a men's night out. I'm buying."

Dov is notoriously cheap.

"You can even come along too," he says to me.

I'm not sure if this is a crack about my age or the length of my hair.

"What did you have in mind?" Abba asks.

"Dinner at the Chinese."

That's what Dov calls the Hungry Lion. It's the only Chinese restaurant in town and Pearl considers it an embarrassment to her people. Terrible lighting. Sticky floors. Peeling posters of the Great Wall in the windows. Most souls brave enough to eat the food only do takeout. But Dov just loves it to pieces.

Mom is thrilled because, for once on a Friday night, she can go to services at Temple Beth Torah.

There's a party tonight I'm not going to because Pearl can't go out. I'll be damned if I'm going to hang out by myself while Zim sneaks off with Maddie Green.

I'm not going even though Rebecca Walsh might be there and I heard she broke up with Dylan, because I figure this whole Younger Brother of a Returning Soldier thing isn't going to get me the right kind of attention from her.

Not that I'd ever use Boaz's story to score with a girl. I'm not that kind of guy. If I were, I'd make more of an effort with Sophie Olsen.

Anyway. I tell Dov to count me in.

"Great." Dov rubs his hands together. Abba's still reading e-mails on his BlackBerry. "What's our ETD?" he asks.

Dov checks his watch. "Nowishly."

"*B'seder.*" Abba still taps away. He doesn't look up from his little device but still manages to direct his next sentence at me.

"Go get your brother."

I sit and pick a thread from the hem of my T-shirt.

"Please?" Abba says.

It's practically unheard of for Abba to even say *please*, and then on top of it he says it in this way that has worry and fear and tenderness all wrapped up in it.

He's not really lost in his work, he's just trying to look like it. He doesn't want to ask Boaz to join us.

He doesn't know how.

I take the stairs slowly. I stop outside his door. Before I can knock, Boaz opens it.

"Looking for this?" He holds out my laptop.

"Thanks." I take it.

He's opened the door enough for me to see that his bed on the floor is made. The clothes and the weights and the papers have all been put away. Everything spotless.

It's like he's opened the door on a room in a parallel universe.

He starts to close the door again, but I brush by him and step inside, figuring the rules might be different in this upside-down world.

"We're going to the Hungry Lion."

Maybe Mom was right. Maybe all he needed was time. Maybe he's coming back around. Maybe that other universe, the one we've been living in, maybe that's the one with the wrong side up.

"Dov and Abba and me," I say. "We're going to the Hungry Lion. It'd be great if you came along."

"I don't know. . . ."

Boaz is edging me out of the room without actually touching me.

"Please, just come with us." Much as I wish it didn't, this *please* comes out sounding an awful lot like Abba's did.

He's herded me back into the hallway. He turns around and looks back into his room the way someone might look at a mountain of work piled high on a neglected desk. He sighs.

"You go ahead."

"Okay." I head back downstairs to face the two people I most hate to disappoint.

But then Bo clears his throat. "I'll catch up with you there."

On the ride Dov puzzles over this. "What? He's taking *your* car?" he asks Abba.

"I don't know."

"I think he just wants to walk," I offer.

"Walk? What kind of *mishugas* is that? It'll take him the better part of an hour."

"Dov," Abba says. "It's okay. If that's what he wants."

At this point Dov makes the switch over to Hebrew and they go back and forth for the rest of the ride and I stare out the window.

We take our time ordering. Service at the Hungry Lion is slow on the best of days, so as it turns out, Boaz arrives just after the food.

He takes a seat and immediately starts filling his plate. He orders a Chinese beer from the waiter. When he last lived at home he was too young to drink, and the ease with which he orders alcohol in public is maybe the most grown-up thing I've ever seen him do with my own two eyes.

Dov is on a tear about a recent rash of theft in his neighborhood. He links it, through his own brand of improbable logic, to the overconsumption of processed foods.

"Ingesting all that crap makes decent people do indecent things."

Abba calls Dov insane.

The night feels normal, almost.

Boaz doesn't say much, but he eats and he watches Abba and Dov go back and forth in their ridiculous argument. Even I've learned by now that Dov sets a trap with his proclamations, but each time, without fail, Abba steps right into it like he's never come across one before.

"So, *motek*," Dov says to Boaz. "Did you get enough to eat?"

"Sure did, Dov."

"Like I said, I'm buying. So if you want to order more . . ."

"I'm good."

Bo shoves his empty plate away from him. Dov stares at it.

"Levi went and got himself a job this summer," Abba says. "He's selling movie tickets."

"No, Abba, I'm working at Videorama. It's a video store. We rent DVDs."

"So why don't they call it a DVD store?" Dov asks.

I don't respond because I know how to skirt a trap.

"Boaz," Abba says carefully. "Any thought about what you might do this summer? If not, I was thinking—"

"Yes."

"Yes, what?"

"I've thought about it."

The entire restaurant goes quiet. Strangers put down their chopsticks. The man at the counter ceases yelling orders to the guys in the kitchen. The fluorescent lights, on their last bit of juice, quit their buzzing.

Okay, so none of this really happens, but that's how things feel to me.

"And?"

"I'm going on a hike."

"For the summer?"

Boaz nods. "The Appalachian Trail."

Abba and Dov exchange a look: *That makes perfect sense.* They turn to Boaz and bob their heads approvingly.

Boaz takes another pull from his beer. I study his face.

Not a hint.

Nothing to give away that what he just said is an absolute lie.

I've seen the maps. The maps Boaz browses online and some he created himself, linking one location to another, on a Web site that lets you do that sort of thing.

I've learned a ton looking at those maps.

I know Boaz prefers the scenic roads, avoiding highways at all costs. He's researched which bridges are pedestrian accessible, where the campsites are and the cheap motels. Boaz connects specific addresses in Connecticut, New Jersey,

Maryland and Washington, DC, into one long ribbon of a route. And he's broken that route down into increments of around twenty miles.

He's done no research whatsoever on the Appalachian Trail.

I know if it came to it, I couldn't prove positively that Boaz is lying, that he *isn't* planning on hiking the Appalachian Trail. I took a logic class last fall. I had to practically hold Zim's hand through the class and painstakingly explain the reading to him. I know what it takes to prove a theory. It's harder than you'd think.

Logic gets me no place when it comes to Boaz. I have only my instincts and some shards of evidence. But still, there are some things a brother knows.

So I know this: he's lying.

And he's pretty damn good at it.

SEVEN

PEARL SERVES ME A SNICKERDOODLE frozen yogurt. I feel about frozen yogurt the way I do about cats and Broadway musicals. I'm not a fan.

"Just eat it," she says. "Make like a paying customer."

"I'm not paying for this."

She sighs. All exasperation. "I know, moron. I just started this job three days ago. I don't want it to look like I'm screwing around in front of Il Duce."

"Huh?"

"The boss. He's kind of intense." She motions toward him over her left shoulder. The kid can't be a day over sixteen. He has the acne to prove it.

"Him?"

She nods.

I take a bite. "This is disgusting."

"Is that why you're bothering me at work? To malign my product?"

"No."

"Well?"

"It's Boaz."

The door opens. It's Zim.

He still doesn't have a job, but he's kept tight track of my schedule. He knows I'm on break and I spend my breaks with Pearl. He orders vanilla. She makes him pay.

Pearl looks at her watch. She does a little curtsy. "Could you take this one, sir? I'm due for my fifteen-minute break."

Il Duce rolls his eyes and steps up to the counter.

The heat outside melts my yogurt.

"*Nu?*" Pearl has picked up some of Abba's vocabulary.

"Yeah," Zim says. "*Nu?*"

"He says he's going to hike the Appalachian Trail."

"That's good, right?" Zim asks.

"It would be if that's what he was really planning on doing."

Pearl lights up a Marlboro. She positions herself facing the entrance, so she can ditch the cancer stick if her boss comes after her.

She takes a deep drag. "So what's his real plan?"

"I don't know. But he's heading south. Stopping all sorts of places. I think he's going to Washington, DC." I take a bite of my yogurt. "Jesus. What's in here anyway?"

"Snickers." She shrugs. "And Doodles." She takes it and throws it into the Dumpster.

"Maybe it's a good thing that he's getting away. That he's going somewhere and doing something." Zim has a yogurt mustache. The guy eats like a child. "So what if he's not hiking the Appalachian Trail?"

"He's lying," I say.

"So? Everybody lies," Pearl says.

"Right. They lie to cover up for something bad."

She stubs out her cigarette. "What's so bad about going to DC?"

"The fact that he has to lie about it."

Suddenly, I'm all agitation. Damp armpits and itchy scalp. I swat at a fly that isn't there.

I'm not sure what's gnawing at me exactly. I haven't played out any worst-case scenarios because I don't really have any to play out. It's just worry, like the kind I always get in the ocean. That uneasy feeling when the tide first starts its tug away from shore.

I sit down on the curb. Pearl and Zim sit on either side of me.

"The weirdest part is, I'm pretty sure he's planning on walking."

"Levi—"

"Please. I can't have another conversation about how he's a hero. So if you're going to say that, or something about how he just needs to do whatever he needs to do, or about how he needs time, or some sort of bullshit like that, please, don't."

"Relax, dude," Zim says. "I was just going to tell you you have snickerdoodles on your shoes."

Pearl reaches over with a corner of her apron and wipes the spot of yogurt off my Vans. She drapes an arm around my shoulder.

"We'll figure this out," she says.

I know this is just Pearl saying one of those things friends say. And I know it doesn't really mean anything. And I know Pearl always does this in the moments when there really isn't anything else to do. But still.

I'm glad to hear her say it.

Mom gets herself all worked up over Boaz's trip. She races out and buys him a sleeping bag made of material she read about in the science section of the *New York Times* that weighs only a few ounces and keeps you warm in the Arctic and cool on the surface of the sun. Or something.

"I went camping one summer with some girlfriends," Mom tells me as she's cooking dinner.

I've offered to peel potatoes.

"It was a gas. I loved being so far away from everything. It's amazing how quickly we can adapt to the absence of all those things we've invented to make our lives more comfortable. I wiped my bottom with big-leaf aster!"

"Mom. Seriously. Gross."

"They're these wonderful big heart-shaped leaves that grow everywhere. Always within arm's reach."

She smiles and salts the boiling water. Some salt spills on the counter and she picks up a pinch and tosses it over her shoulder.

Sure. Like that'll keep her bad luck at bay.

She chuckles to herself. "Big-leaf aster. I never quite got how funny that sounds when you consider what it is we were doing with it."

I have to admit it's good to see Mom happy. We haven't spent time like this, talking in the kitchen, since I can remember. Some of that has to be my fault. When was the last time I offered to peel potatoes?

This is how it should be. Now that he's back, this is how it should be. We should stand around the kitchen and laugh. We should talk about stupid things that don't matter too much.

Here we are, finally, where we should be, and now he's planning on leaving us again.

"This is going to be so great for Bo." Mom dumps the peeled potatoes into the water. "I've always wanted to hike the Appalachian Trail. Once, I suggested it to your father, that we take a family trip, just a long weekend, but he thought you were too young. He didn't want to have to carry you on his shoulders the whole time."

"Sorry I blew your plans."

"Don't be silly. You would have been fine. Abba was wrong. You've always been tough. A little go-getter. You would've kept up and probably led the way."

I'm not quite sure who she's talking about. It certainly doesn't sound anything like the me I know.

"Anyway," she continues, "I think this might be just what our Boaz needs. A chance to get his head on straight. To let go of everything. To worry about nothing but the sounds of the birds in the trees or how to heat up a can of beans over an open fire."

"I think he's planning on being gone for quite a while," I say carefully. I'm torn between wanting to prolong Mom's good mood and wanting to lay everything out on the table.

"So?" she shoots back. "Don't you think he's earned himself a vacation?"

She breathes in through her nose and starts her gentle humming.

"Mom?"

"Yes?" She turns her back to me. Busy at the stove.

"Nothing."

Maybe it's better for her, for us all, to imagine him on vacation. Walking nature's glorious paths. Wiping his ass with big, soft leaves.

Let us imagine him warm in the Arctic and cool on the surface of the sun.

We'll stay right where we are. Right where we've been.

Waiting.

All those trips to his room. Running my hands over his possessions. I never once took anything. Not a penny. Not a pair of socks. Not an old piece of Halloween candy.

Nothing.

Until now.

The way I've looked into Bo's online history, the way I've scoured his maps, and now, the way I've uncovered the password that allows me access to his e-mail—I just don't see how you can call it anything but theft.

It's no different from when I used to steal Twix bars from the supermarket on my way home from fifth grade, except that then I felt only slightly guilty.

Now I feel a big sort of guilt.

A grown man's guilt.

But I also feel like I've been driven to steal, which I know sounds a lot like blaming the victim.

I mean, I can't say the Price Chopper had it coming. No amount of bad Muzak or frigid temperatures gives someone the right to steal a Twix bar. But the way Boaz has been, the way he's acted since he's been home, the way he went off and wrote us all out of the story of his life, the way his behavior would lead any reasonable person to want to understand more, all I'm saying is: he kind of asked for it.

So yes, I blame the victim.

His password is *PAR-PAR*.

At first I have no idea what this means. I try to see if there's some numeric equivalent. Like the way I tell people my cell number is the UGLY Hotline because the last four digits, 8459, spell out *UGLY* on a phone.

PAR-PAR. 727-727

Is it an important date? Part of his social security number? Does this have something to do with airplanes?

I spend a good hour like this because that's the way my mind works. I'm more a numbers guy than someone who's clever with words.

Finally I stick it into my search engine.

I run it through the same translation program I use when Abba swears in Hebrew.

And there it is.

Parpar. The Hebrew word for butterfly.

Christina calls and asks me to meet her for a cup of coffee.

I can't because I've got a checkup with the pediatrician I've had since birth, the one with the Barney poster on his wall I stare at while he cradles my balls in his hairy, spotted old man's hand. So naturally I lie and tell her I've got to work. We make a plan for the following afternoon.

When the waitress comes by our table I order a cappuccino and immediately regret it when Christina orders a cup of black coffee.

"Listen," she says. "I want you to know that I'm going to Washington. Max got a summer associate position at a big law firm there."

Washington? Why is everyone going to Washington?

That's what I think.

But what I say is "Really?"

"In the tax department."

"You must be so proud."

She eyes me. I figure she must be getting used to my weird, unjustified jealousy by now, just like I'm starting to accept the fact that no matter how pathetic I come off, I can't seem to keep my mouth shut.

"Actually, I am," she says. "Quite proud. There are all sorts of ways to lead a decent, meaningful life."

"*Parpar*," I say.

Her jaw drops. Her eyes widen. She leans in closer. She whispers, "What did you say?"

"Nothing."

I don't need to say anything else. I have my answer.

"No, really, what was that?"

"Nothing."

She tries staring me down but then she gives. She shakes it off like you would some trick of the light.

"Look, I *am* sorry. Sorry to be leaving right now. I don't

even know what sort of help I could have been, but regardless, I'm sorry I won't be here."

"It's okay, Christina. Boaz is leaving too."

"He is?"

"Yes."

"Are you going to tell me where he's going?" She stirs her coffee slowly.

I take a sip of my cappuccino. "He's going to hike the Appalachian Trail."

EIGHT

MOM GOES ON A CRAZY SHOPPING SPREE.

That magic sleeping bag. An equally high-tech tent. An ergonomically designed backpack. Drip-dry pants. A bundle of socks. She picks up two guidebooks to the Appalachian Trail. One with foldout maps.

She buys three pairs of hiking boots for Boaz to try on in the comfort of his own home.

She doesn't make much of his refusal to accompany her to the store. He's pretty clear about not wanting to drive and she seems to accept this like it's no big deal. Just another item on her list of Bo's little peculiarities, like his double-jointed thumb or his birthmark the shape of Texas.

She spreads her purchases out on the dining room table.

"So? Whaddya think?"

I've just come in from a run. I'm on my way upstairs to stretch.

"Looks good, Mom."

Clearly, this isn't the reaction she wants.

"You know, it wouldn't kill you to take a little more interest."

"What am I supposed to say?" I shoot back. "Nice mosquito netting?"

She waves me off. "Forget about it."

Right then Abba walks in. Home early from work.

"How far?" he barks.

"About twelve miles."

"*B'seder.* Maybe next year you'll try out for cross-country."

"Okay," I say, even though I won't. Not a chance. But I'm not used to Abba weighing in on what I should do with my life, and I've forgotten the words to tell him no.

Abba gestures to Mom's table. "What's with all this?"

"It's stuff for Bo's trip."

She starts showing him the boots, the sleeping bag, the water-resistant socks. She's acting like a hostess on a game show. *All these items can be yours!*

I watch Abba turn things over in his hands. They seem to have forgotten I'm here, and that probably means Mom has forgotten she's mad at me, and that's good, right?

And now I can just go upstairs and listen to music and stretch after my run and forget about it, but watching this little show, and all the pleasure Mom is taking in all this stuff, I'm getting pissed.

Suddenly, I'm taking the stairs two at a time and I'm pounding on Boaz's door. I'm not lightly tapping, or scratching with my chewed-down nails.

It's not an *I'm so sorry to bother you* knock. It's an OPEN THE FUCKING DOOR NOW knock.

Once he undoes the latch I push my way in. Bo steps aside and I spin around on him.

"What are you doing?" I ask.

"What are *you* doing?"

Boaz backs his way into his desk chair and folds one leg over the other. I have no place to sit because his mattress is still on the floor, and he's in the only chair, and the absence of this choice, of any place to sit down and talk to him at eye level, leaves me with this wild, untethered feeling.

"I'm trying to find out what's up with this whole Appalachian Trail thing."

"I'm going hiking," Bo says calmly.

"No you aren't."

"I'm not?"

"No. You're not. I know you're not. You aren't going anywhere near the Appalachian Trail."

Bo scoffs at me. It's the closest he's come to smiling since I can remember. "What do you know?"

"Is this some sort of joke to you? Is it? Because Mom's down with half the stock of the Outdoor Store sprawled across the dining room table, and she's practically doing cartwheels she's so amped up. All over a trip you aren't actually taking."

I finally settle for a corner of the mattress on the floor. I don't know what to do with my legs, so I pull them to my chest in a pose that's undeniably childlike.

"What are you up to, Boaz? Huh? I mean, what are you planning? Where are you going? Why?"

"Levi. Lemme give you some advice." He leans in closer like he's about to share a secret with me.

Then his voice goes cold. Sharp.

"Stay out of this."

It's a voice I don't know, but it's one I'm sure he's put to good use over the last three years. And to avoid it, and the way he's looking at me, I stare at the wall over what used to be his bed.

It's empty.

"Where's my map?"

"Can you leave now?"

"I want my map."

"Get out."

I stop looking at his e-mails. I stop scouring his maps. I'd like to tell you that I came to this decision in a moment of clarity, that I realized how wrong I'd been to stalk Bo's online trail.

What a violation.

How unbrotherly.

But the real truth is that I didn't come to this decision: Boaz did.

He returns my computer after canceling his e-mail account and erasing his online history. He isn't just covering his tracks. He's ended the trail altogether.

Zim comes to visit me at work. He's still looking around for a job. His dream of spending the summer with his hands deep in women's hair didn't pan out. It kills me, because Zim has an encyclopedic knowledge of film. He deserved this job. He should be the one sitting behind the counter eating microwave popcorn all day.

He rubs his hands together. "Time to start planning the big one."

He hops up on the counter and dangles his legs off the side. Bob never seems to mind Zim hanging around. He cuts me a lot of slack. I can see it in the way he looks at me. That mixture of deference and respect. Like by living down the hall from my brother, I've caught a bit of his heroism, the way one might catch a cold.

"What're you talking about?" I ask Zim.

"Our eighteenth birthday, my Birthday Brotha. In the eyes of many, we will, at long last, be men."

Oh, right. Our birthdays are only a few weeks away. Thank God I've already gotten the ball-cradling checkup out of the way.

"Let's do something seriously raging this year. Something to prove ourselves worthy of the right to vote and smoke."

"And join the military."

"Right."

A silence follows. I've deflated poor Zim.

"He leaves tomorrow?" he asks.

"Yep. Tomorrow."

"And still no idea what he's up to?"

"Nope."

"Maybe he'll prove you wrong. Maybe he's really off to hike the Trail."

I sigh. "Yeah, maybe."

Zim wanders off to browse the horror section.

I hate being a downer, but I don't care much about what birthday is on my horizon, and for sure, I don't feel much like a man.

● ● ●

I try to remember if we had a farewell dinner before Bo left for boot camp. If we did, it was nothing like this. No festivity. Tonight Mom's got the Beatles on in the kitchen and she's singing along and I'm thinking how much it burns when your mom loves the same music you do.

I'm also thinking that maybe I should forget what I know.

Zim could be right. Maybe Boaz will prove me wrong. I should just put aside all that logic, tuck into Mom's farewell dinner and believe in the Appalachian Trail.

It seems to be working just fine for everyone else.

Take Abba. He comes home, arms full of wine. He's crazy about his wines. Special occasions call for wines he spends real money on, and that means you'd better brace for a long speech about oaks and tannins.

He likes to make me taste the ones he's most excited about.

"Delicious," I say, even though to me, wine tastes like grassy Band-Aids.

Dov comes over with a special package for Boaz.

"It's from Mr. Kurjian," he says. "An Armenian lunch for your first day on the trail."

"Thanks, Dov." Without looking inside, he puts the bag in the refrigerator.

"You all set?"

"Think so."

"How about some cash?" Dov reaches for his wallet.

Sometimes he acts like a crisp twenty-dollar bill is the answer to all life's troubles.

"Nah. I'm good."

"You sure?"

The way Dov narrows his eyes at him, I question what he believes.

"I'm sure, Dov."

We sit down to eat. I swirl the little bit of wine around and around in a comically oversized glass. I take a deep whiff. Then a sip. "Delicious."

All through dinner and dessert, through the several glasses Abba fills for him with expensive wine, Boaz never once looks in my direction.

With cottony eyes I make out the red digital numbers.

Five. Five. Seven.

The buzzer on this very same clock usually fails to wake me, but this morning, at this obscene hour, the gentle click of Boaz shutting the front door behind him does the job.

I climb out of bed, scramble down the hallway, enter my brother's empty room and head straight for the window facing the street.

I pull up the shade to a soft pink sky.

Somehow he looks small under the weight of all his things. He's walking down the painted white dashes that divide the two sides of the road. There's no traffic to contend with. All the world is sleeping.

I watch him go. Wondering if he'll bother to look back. Not sure what I'd do if he did.

Wave? Or duck so I couldn't be seen? Maybe I'd shout out his name. Wake the birds and the neighbors.

Maybe I'd find something to tell my brother, finally. Something important. One of those things people say at life's big moments. The kind of thing that makes you think: *I'll remember that.*

Maybe those sorts of words would find their way onto my tongue.

Maybe.

Boaz reaches the corner. His final chance to turn back and look.

I close my eyes tight. Shield myself from a glare only I can see. When I open them again, Boaz is gone.

I sit on the floor of his room and dig my hands into his carpet.

I imagine his path through the neighborhood. Even with everything he's been through, with as far away as he's gone from here and how he returned some other version of himself, he must still know these streets.

These are our streets.

He just turned up Archer, where I took the first spin on my bike without training wheels. Then he'll go down Lincoln, where when I was seven, Abba broke the news that the family dog died, his face sad and serious. On Burr Street, where he'll start heading south, Mom told me that Dov was in the hospital, but not to worry, he's an ox. He'll be okay. And then Pierce Avenue, where Abba tried out his lame version of the "sex talk" and I pretended what he said might have some relevance in my natural lifetime.

Come to think of it, most of the important conversations I've had in my life took place while walking these streets. Walking, like running, gives your body something to do while your head is reeling.

Soon he'll leave the neighborhood. He'll start heading west on a complex combination of the less-traveled roads, the ones friendlier to someone with nothing but a backpack and a pair of fancy boots.

I know where he's headed. I've seen the maps. I've read some e-mails.

First to Poughkeepsie, to meet up with a guy named Loren, who I first mistook for a girl. That would make sense to me. Walking across three states for the love of a beautiful girl.

But no.

Loren is a guy, someone Boaz served with, judging from the nature of their e-mails. Honestly, I barely get what they're talking about, and maybe someone else would say the same thing about an exchange of messages between me and Zim, or me and Pearl, but this feels different.

Anyway, the one thing I do understand is that Loren doesn't know what Boaz is up to any more than I do, because when he asked, Boaz just said he's *passing through Poughkeepsie*.

I figure it should take him around nine days to get there. That's if he walks about twenty miles a day.

I go back over the neighborhood walks of my past. The ones where I'm sorting through some difficult piece of news. I always had someone next to me, someone to talk to. And it kills me that Boaz, even if he is the King of Silence himself, is on this walk alone.

I stand up and go back to my room. I'm hoping to drift back to sleep, though I'm pretty sure that won't happen. I climb into bed, pull up the covers and brush up against a foreign object.

I've lived my entire life sleeping alone in this bed, so the presence of something next to me, anything next to me, delivers quite the shock.

It's tucked under the covers, on the side of my bed closest to the wall. I reach for it—a long, rolled-up piece of paper wrapped in a rubber band, frayed around the edges. I slide off the rubber band and unfurl it slowly. In the dim light of my room, my eyes take their time adjusting.

Pastel-colored states and baby-blue oceans swim into view.

My old Rand McNally map.

Boaz must have snuck in here in the dark—maybe he padded across my rug in his tube-socked feet.

I stare at the map while the sun comes up. Boaz didn't take the time to erase his pencil scrawlings. They practically fill the Atlantic.

Are they clues? Is this an invitation? Does he want me to know where he's going? Does he want me to find him? Stop him? Join him?

Or is he simply giving me back what I demanded, like a whiny little brother?

I roll up the map. I stash it under my bed.

I never go back to sleep.

NINE

I SIT INSIDE VIDEORAMA ALL DAY, alone but for Bob and the fake buttery smell of microwave popcorn.

Outside in the world people are swimming in creeks. They're riding bikes, maybe giving a friend a lift on the front handlebars. Somewhere out there a boy is gearing up to kiss a girl for the very first time. Maybe on a camp tennis court, in the fading light of day, to a chorus of just-stirring crickets.

Outside someone is walking toward something.

For something.

Because of something.

I don't mean to romanticize the messed-up world of my brother, but any way you cut it, as I sit in here running the scanner over bar codes and calculating change for a twenty, I'm wasting the minutes away.

And then I have this revelation that is so totally not a revelation, because I'm pretty sure revelations are supposed to rock your world to the core and this is the most obvious thing ever, but here goes: There's more to do. More I can do. There is more than this.

● ● ●

I race to Frozurt on my lunch break.

I've discovered I'm able to stomach the peach, if it's the price of spending time with Pearl. She readies my order when she sees me walk in. Granola on top.

"You better eat quick," she says. "I don't think Il Duce much likes your lunchtime visits."

"So what?"

"So we don't want to make him angry. Nobody likes Il Duce when he's angry."

I can see him sitting in the back office, in a swivel chair, talking on the phone and folding paper airplanes.

Pearl leans over the counter. "How's your day going?"

This isn't idle talk. She's asking something bigger. How is *this* day going?

The fifth since he's been gone.

I tell her how I woke to an empty house. It's not unusual for Abba to rise early and head in to work. He's not the type to linger over the paper and a cup of coffee. But today Mom was gone too. She left a note on the table.

Off to interview for a freelance thing.

Waffles in the fridge.

So I tell Pearl that waffles don't belong in the fridge, and Mom doesn't belong at a job interview. Both disrupt the natural world order.

"I guess it's time," Pearl says. "She's no longer got any business sitting home worrying. And besides, the pay is lousy."

"She's got plenty of reason to sit home and worry."

"She might, but fortunately, she doesn't know it."

"But I do."

"Yes, you do."

"And I'm going to do something about it."

When I get home from work there's a letter waiting for me.

The letter is from Christina Crowley.

I take it up to my room and lock the door behind me. I climb out onto the roof. I hold it in my hands and stare at my name in her handwriting.

I don't want to open it right away.

I want to know what it feels like to sit with an unopened letter from Christina Crowley in my lap.

I slowly slide my finger under the back flap of the envelope and take out a single sheet of white paper. I unfold it with the precision experts must use in dismantling a bomb.

What do I expect?

A whiff of perfume? A lipstick kiss? A declaration of her undying love in feminine cursive?

Or maybe what I'm hoping for is all those sad little things—perfume, kiss, cursive—not for me, but for my brother, like somehow she'd find it necessary to communicate to me that her love for him didn't die when he chose to leave her for a war.

What I read instead is a note. All business: Here's how to reach me in Washington if you need to. Here's my e-mail, my new cell phone number and the address where I'll be living, it's a studio in Georgetown, with Max.

• • •

On day eight I go for a run.

Mom started a new job. She's doing graphic design for an advertising firm. Two months is all she'd commit to. By then she figures, Bo will be back, brand-new digital camera filled up with pictures of the Appalachian Trail. By then she figures, maybe he'll need her.

Dusk's arrival hasn't done much to cool off the day. About every other house has its sprinkler system on, and I go out of my way to run through the drops of water, which disappear from my skin as quickly as they land.

I run through the same streets Boaz took on his way out of the neighborhood, but when I get to the intersection where his route went west, I turn the other way, in toward familiar places.

This is the way to school. To Pearl's. This is the way into Boston, where I go sometimes when I need a reminder that the world isn't tiny. That there are places where people look at you just because you happen to be walking by, not because they think they know something about who you are, or what you've been through.

I come up on my school. The gate to the athletic field is open.

I run down to the track and knock off eight laps. Two miles. I'm pretty sure this is what guys on the track team do. They run around in circles. Around and around with no place to go. It starts to do my head in, all those circles, so I leave. Back through the gate, out onto the street, and up toward the front of the school.

The streetlamps have switched on even though it isn't all that dark yet. Big pools of yellow light scatter down the sidewalk ahead of me. I'm closing in on the main building.

We've been out a few weeks now. The front of the school is deserted except for one car.

I don't have to get any closer to see that I know this car. Not as well as Dov's lime-green Caprice Classic, but that's only because Dov's car was my first, and cars, like I imagine it must be with girls, leave their mark on you.

I slow to a walk and try to catch my breath before approaching from the rear.

I made that dent in the left bumper, and afterward Mom wouldn't let me drive her car for a week.

Something must be terribly wrong.

Why else would she come out in this disappearing dusk to look for me? When has Mom ever come looking for me?

I catch my breath but my pulse won't slow. I stand for a minute, thinking maybe she'll see me in the rearview mirror. Then I notice her head in her hands. Her body is shaking.

I come up on the passenger side. I rap the glass lightly. She jumps, but then she sees it's me. She fumbles for the button on her door and unrolls the window. She wipes her eyes with a tissue she pulls from her purse.

"What are you doing here?" she asks.

I crouch down and lean on the doorframe. "You aren't looking for me?"

She shakes her head and then blows her nose. She reaches for her keys and finally turns off the ignition. I open the passenger door and climb into the car, moving her new briefcase to the floor by my feet.

"If you aren't looking for me, what are you . . ."

I stop once I catch a glimpse of her view through the windshield. School's out. Nobody's around. Summer's in full swing. Another class has graduated and gone on to start bright futures, but rather than wishing them well, those magnetic letters on the sign in front of the school still welcome Boaz home.

"I'm sorry," she says.

"For what?"

"For this." She gestures to the wadded-up Kleenex on the floor of her car. To her tear-streaked face. "I know I should be happy. I should feel relieved. Lucky. We *are* lucky. So incredibly lucky. I know that. I know there are mothers everywhere, all over this country, all over this world, who would give anything to trade places with me. Who would love the chance to cry because they're *worried* about their sons. There are mothers lost in the wilds of their own grief, who miss the days of worrying. I know. I know worrying is far better than grieving. But, God help me, sometimes I don't know the difference. I can't separate the grief from the worry."

"Mom." I know I should say more, but in some way it's as if I'm not even here. Like anyone could have stumbled into this passenger seat in his sweaty running gear and caught her soliloquy.

She's talking to herself, or to the universe, more than she is to me. But it's good. It's good. Because Mom isn't as clueless as I thought she was.

"It's good," I mumble.

She looks at me sideways. She checks her face in the mirror and wipes away the mascara trails from her cheeks.

"You know, this is so far from how I imagined things would turn out, sometimes it seems I'm living someone else's life."

"I think I know the feeling."

She leans back into the driver's seat. "I never let you boys play with guns or toy soldiers when you were little. When Boaz was a baby, I dressed him in pink striped pajamas. I fed you hot dogs without sulfites. I thought I was doing everything right."

"You did, Mom. Look." I point to the sign. "He's an *American Hero*. You must have done *something* right."

"I know. It's just . . . this isn't what I wanted for him. I never wanted *this*. And now, I just want him back."

"He'll be back."

She searches my face until she sees me.

"Where do you think he is, Levi? I mean, where do you think he is right this minute?"

I have no idea if she's testing me. If this is my chance to share what little I know. Or what little I think I know.

"I gave him a cell phone," she adds. "A new one. But he doesn't turn it on."

No, this isn't my chance. It's not what she wants, and sometimes, I guess, it's just better to do what someone wants of you.

"Mom, there's probably no reception on the trail. I'm sure when he gets somewhere with service, he'll check in."

She nods. She looks up at the sign. Her lips move, just the slightest bit, as she reads those words over to herself again.

"Where is he?" she whispers.

All the light has left the sky. The yellow streetlamps make a pathetic effort to tame the darkness.

"I think maybe he's lying in his new sleeping bag," I tell her. "I think he's waiting on the stars."

TEN

I'M SITTING IN HIS ROOM. On his bed. The mattress is back on the frame now. I can picture Mom, struggling underneath its unwieldy size.

I can see the marks on the wall from where he taped up my Rand McNally map before returning it to me in the dead of night. His computer, with its broken motherboard, still sits on his desk. The radio, quiet, tucked on the shelf between a set of barbells and books with worn-out spines.

I'm cataloging the place. Trying to make some sense out of everything by figuring out what's here and what's gone.

He's gone.

That I know. He took those printed out maps. And all the new stuff Mom bought for him except for the cell phone. I found it, still in its package, behind a row of shoes in his closet. That box from Marty Muldoon's is nowhere to be found. I know because I looked for it everywhere.

I roll out my Rand McNally map, pin it to the bed and stare at it.

I could wait for the second destination. Or the one after

that. He has all sorts of addresses scribbled into the baby-blue Atlantic.

Or I could go now. Today. Tomorrow might even be safe. If I go soon, I could catch up with him in Poughkeepsie.

There was a short period after Boaz left for boot camp when I imagined that as soon as I turned eighteen I'd follow him. I'd walk the path he'd blazed. I'd get fitted for a uniform. Pummeled into a muscled physique. Shaved close to the scalp.

This wasn't because I wanted to become a marine. And it certainly wasn't because I believed, like Boaz did, that part of becoming a man is fighting for your country. It was as simple as me assuming, as I had all my life, that someday I'd be like my brother. That I'd follow right behind him.

I got over that quickly enough. I grew out my hair. Took up smoking. Once Boaz was gone, I started feeling my way through a life outside of my brother's shadow, only to learn that shadows grow even bigger when cast from half a world away.

It's today, I decide. It has to be today.

I cross the street to Zim's but he isn't home. I look around back, figuring I might find him shooting baskets. Nope. Propped up against the garage I see Zim's old skateboard, and I grab it. It's the same one he used to ride back in the days when there was nothing more important to either of us than skateboarding. I don't even have a board anymore, and I figure that's part of my problem. Not that I don't skate, but that nothing ever took its place. There's nothing in my life as important to me as skateboarding once was.

I ride Zim's board over to Pearl's. Mama Goldblatt answers the door.

I don't have a thing for women in their late forties, but if I did, I'd be totally hot for Mama Goldblatt. She's smart and beautiful, and she's got some big job at the public television station where she produces shows on world music and culture, and I know how Pearl likes to pretend her mother is totally lame and out of touch, but the truth is, if Pearl grows up to be one half as hip as Mama Goldblatt, she'll be doing just fine.

"Levi. Darling," she says in her deep lullaby voice. "How *are* you?"

It's the first I've seen her in weeks.

"I'm okay."

"And your brother, he's home now?"

"Not exactly."

"No?"

"He was here, but now he's left again."

"He got called back?"

"No, no. He's just gone off to, like, collect himself."

"Oh. That doesn't sound so good."

Here's another thing about Mama Goldblatt: she's got a serious rack, or as Mom likes to call it, an "ample bosom."

There's something about her, and I don't think it's just her chest, that makes me want to tell her everything. When I'm around her I fight the urge to crack myself open like an overripe melon, and it's lucky for Pearl I fear her wrath more than I'm undone by Mama Goldblatt's lullaby voice, or else by now I'd have shared Pearl's secrets, and Mama Goldblatt might have locked her away in a real convent.

"Is Pearl here?"

"Out back. But grab something from the kitchen first. She tells me you've been living off a diet of peach frozen yogurt."

Pearl is reading in the sun under a ridiculously large hat. She shrugs. "What can I say? I burn easily."

"I need a ride."

"Where?"

"Poughkeepsie."

"Isn't Poughkeepsie like three hours away?"

"About."

"I'm due at work in forty-five minutes."

"Maybe it's time for a sick day."

She thinks this over. "I do love the dramatic prospect in that idea."

"Have I mentioned that you're looking a little peaked?"

She coughs. Rubs her temples. She groans. Then she coughs again. "How'd that sound?"

"Perfect."

We take I-90, which couldn't possibly be a less interesting route. I-90 is nothing but a big slab of concrete cutting the state of Massachusetts in two, and here we are, barreling down it. The very act of driving down the interstate seems so absurdly unsafe suddenly. We're just suckers in a little cocoon made of tin.

Every choice we make is a risk. Every single choice.

Pearl puts in a CD she made for road trips. She'd had it sitting on her shelf for over three years. This is the first chance she's had to play it. Two songs in and she pops it out again.

"Jesus, I had bad taste at fourteen."

"Didn't we all."

I have the address and directions folded into my lap. So much information, one small click away. If only there were a Web site that could answer the *why* of it all.

"Has it occurred to you," Pearl asks, "even if only a little, that maybe Boaz actually *is* hiking the Appalachian Trail, and that we're going to show up unannounced on the doorstep of some guy named Laura who'll look at us like we're totally insane?"

"Loren."

"Whatever."

"Yeah. It has. But if I'm wrong at least you learned your road trip mix sucks the big one."

"True that. Another question, if I may."

"Go on."

"What makes you think he's going to come home with us?"

It's not as if I haven't thought about this. I've thought about it plenty. It's just that I don't get anywhere with that thinking except back to the floor of my room staring at my toes.

In other words: nowhere.

I shrug. "It's a shot in the dark, I guess."

"Better than not taking any shot at all."

That's why I love Pearl.

We trade in I-90 for the Taconic Parkway. A major improvement. Still no walker's road, but pleasant enough. Only two lanes in either direction lined with trees full to bursting.

Pearl lights a cigarette and the smell turns my stomach. I haven't had much to eat today. I open the window and stick my head into the oncoming rush of air like a golden retriever.

We find the address without any trouble. It's a big house, peeling white paint and three stories, sitting at the end of a cul-de-sac, an American flag hanging from the front porch.

Pearl is dying for a pee. We haven't stopped since Framingham. We get out of the car. I do a big stretch and freeze right in the middle of it. For the first time since this whole plan occurred to me, I'm hit hard by fear.

Not a creeping fear.

A paralyzing, didn't-even-know-it-was-coming-and-now-I-can't-move kind of fear.

But then Pearl comes over and links her arm in mine, and that fear starts to recede. She whisks me up the porch steps to the front door, where one of the two buzzers is marked with the name L. Cowell. She pushes it before I have a chance to hesitate. She pushes it three times.

"C'mon, c'mon . . ." She's hopping up and down.

I go back to that exercise we learned in yoga. I close my eyes and try to imagine myself in my safe place. I try picturing the slope of my roof, a warm evening, Pearl stretched out next to me.

Instead what I see when I close my eyes is a fist punching me full in the face. I've never taken a punch to the face, but I always suspected it isn't like it looks in the movies. Guys always get up and go about the fighting in the movies. They stand up. Shake it off. Wipe the blood from the corners of their mouths and then, with narrowed eyes, dig in harder. But I'm pretty sure I'd be done for. Leveled flat. Game over.

"Hello?" A voice on the intercom.

"Hi." Pearl waves, not seeming to care that there's no camera attached to the speaker. "I gotta pee."

I push Pearl out of the way and step closer.

"Hello?"

My voice cracks and I sound like a Girl Scout making her cookie rounds.

"Um, I'm looking for Boaz? Boaz Katznelson? I'm his brother."

The door buzzes. Pearl pulls it open and we stand faced with another door and a narrow staircase.

"Up here," the voice calls.

The stairs are creaky and the carpeting stained. We make our way up two flights. By the time we reach the top, Pearl is out of breath.

Loren stands in the doorframe wearing nothing but plaid boxers and a white T-shirt. If I'd had any question about how Boaz knows him, which I didn't, the haircut is a dead giveaway.

"Hi," Pearl says. "I know you don't know me. But I seriously have to urinate."

"Come on in."

He points her toward the bathroom. I step in behind her. The ceiling is low and slanted and the place feels like an attic hideout. The kind of spot I'd have died to go as a kid and pretend I was all grown up.

"You're Bo's brother?" he asks like he doesn't quite believe this could possibly be true.

"Yeah. Levi."

There doesn't seem to be any air-conditioning. All the heat from the whole massive house gathers in this tiny collection of rooms.

"So, Levi. What are you doing here?"

Sweating. I'm sweating. That's what I'm doing here.

"I'm looking for Boaz."

"I hate to break it to you, but you've come to the wrong place."

"He's not here?"

"Nope." Loren disappears and returns pulling a pair of shorts up over his massive thighs. I guess it finally occurs to him that when meeting people for the first time, it's advisable not to do so in your underwear.

Pearl comes out of the bathroom. "My bladder and I thank you."

"Can I get you guys something to drink?"

I sit down on a small and wildly uncomfortable sofa.

"I'm sorry," I say. "We don't mean to . . . I don't know . . . I just thought he was . . ." I put my head in my hands. "Shit."

"Water would be nice," Pearl says. Loren heads for the kitchen. She sits down next to me and leans in close. "I guess we should have called first."

"Ya think?"

She pokes me hard in the ribs. "You owe me gas money."

Loren returns with two lukewarm waters and a cold beer for himself. He settles himself into the chair facing us. He's far too tall for the low ceilings. Too big for his chair. There are many traits Loren possesses that any reasonable person might find menacing: shoulders like a cow's hindquarters, permanent scowl, deep-set eyes and a scar from his eyebrow to his scalp.

If it weren't for the fact that the cups he poured our water into have bright purple flowers on them, I might just hightail it out of here leaving nothing but a cloud of dust in my wake.

Instead I say, "Sorry to turn up like this, I know it's kinda weird, but, you see, there's this map . . . well, lots of maps, and your address was in the ocean, and there were some e-mails, and I thought I knew—even though he wouldn't tell me anything, I was pretty sure I knew, at least I knew *this*, that he'd be here—but I guess I was wrong."

Loren takes a long drink of his beer.

Pearl sits forward. "What Levi's trying to say, and forgive him, he can get a little tongue-tied, is that he thought Boaz was here and he's a little surprised to find that he's not."

Loren begins to peel the label off his sweating beer bottle.

"Nope. He's not here." He gestures around the living area as if we need some physical proof. Then he sits back deeper into his chair and cracks a smile. "But I didn't say he wasn't here before."

"He was?" I jump up from the sofa like I've got someplace to go and quick. Like maybe if I start running fast enough I might be able to catch him.

"Sit down, junior," Loren says.

I sit.

"So, whaddya want with Bo?"

I stare at him and his marine haircut. I know Dov has plenty to say when it comes to my hair and what sort of signal it sends about me, but that's different. Nobody with hair like Loren's could ever be anything but a marine. His haircut announces, without any room for misunderstanding, exactly who he is.

"I want him to come home."

"Why?"

"Because he needs to. It's time."

"Levi," Loren asks me, "what do you know about the Marines?"

"Nothing, really."

"Exactly."

He leans back in his chair, like Abba does when he's just put me in checkmate. He rolls his beer bottle slowly back and forth over the vast plain of his forehead.

"You see," he continues, "you don't know. You never *will* know. Whoever this guy Boaz was, this brother you thought you knew, he's a marine now. He'll always be a marine. Even if he wishes it weren't so, he can't undo it. It's in his blood. Nobody can undo it."

When Boaz left for training in California, he sent home a shirt for me, athletic gray with the letters USMC across the front. He must have bought the smallest size he could, but still, I swam in that shirt. I only wore it to sleep in, and by the time I grew big enough that I didn't look absurd in it, I still wore it only to sleep in. I never once wore it out in public.

That U and S and M and C—those letters were blue, but to me, for reasons I couldn't quite understand, they felt scarlet.

"How long was he here?" I ask.

"Not too long."

"Where did he go?"

"Why would I tell you that?"

"Because I want to help him. I want him to come home. I want everything to be normal again."

Loren laughs. "That would be nice, wouldn't it?"

He stands up and goes into the kitchen for another beer and I go perfectly still until the sound of the bottle cap separating from the bottle, that small *clink* and the *whoosh* coming from a room away, rattles me like the loudest clap of thunder.

Loren returns and resumes his seat.

"That your girlfriend?"

He nods in Pearl's direction. I've practically forgotten she's here.

"No, I'm not," she answers. "And my name is Pearl."

"That's good news, Pearl. Because girlfriends, at least the ones I know, are nothing but bitches."

I stand up. "Okay. I think it's time for us to get going."

Loren doesn't take his eyes from Pearl. "I don't mean any disrespect, Pearl. Really. You seem like a very nice person. It's just that once you become someone's girlfriend, you become a liar. It's just a fact. You become someone who can no longer be trusted."

"What makes you so sure you can trust me now?" She smiles at him. Flirting, almost. He smiles back.

I stood up with such confidence, such conviction, but

now I sit back down on the sofa with something closer to feebleness. Pearl doesn't need me to stand up for her. She's perfectly capable of doing that herself while remaining fully seated.

"Bo had a girlfriend, didn't he? What was her name again?"

"Christina."

"Right, Christina," Loren says. "Another first-rate, world-class bitch."

I take to my feet again. Pearl might not need me to stand up for her. But Christina? Christina needs me.

I fix Loren with the meanest look I can muster. "You don't know what you're talking about."

"Sure I do. They're all the same. None of them can handle waiting around for their men to come home. Christina was no different."

"Can you blame her? She was eighteen. She thought he was making a mistake. And he was so far away. None of that could've been easy for her."

"It's all a sack of lies."

"You don't know her."

"I know girlfriends. She found someone else. You can count on that. That's why she dumped him. Not because of some bullshit reason about being far away. She jumped in bed with the first chickenshit loser who came along. They all do."

"Oh, right," Pearl says. "And I'm sure you military men are the kinds of boyfriends we girls dream about."

Beyond the haircut, I can't see anything in Loren that reminds me of my brother. Or at least what I know of him. I don't understand how Boaz and this thick-thighed person before me possibly could have been close enough that Boaz would choose to walk to this house, to sleep on this uncomfortable sofa.

Why would he let this person in on his plans, his secrets, when he has a family who loves him, who misses him, who wants to be let in but instead gets the closed bedroom door?

"So." My throat catches and I clear it. "Where's he headed next? New Jersey?"

Loren slowly shifts his gaze from Pearl to me, with effort, like he's got weights on his eyelids. "What makes you think that?"

"The next address is in New Jersey." Off his look I add, "It's written in the ocean."

"I see."

It's time to get out of here. It's been time to get out of here since Pearl took a pee. Every minute since has been a total waste of time.

I want nothing in this entire world but to be free of this apartment and its hot-as-hell, claustrophobic rooms.

Who is this person, anyway?

"Let's go, Pearl," I say.

She sighs dramatically. She puts her palms flat on either side of her and makes like she's about to push herself up. "It was so nice to meet you, Loren. An absolute pleasure."

"He's not going to come home with you," he says, sinking deeper into his chair, stretching his legs out so far in front of him his bare feet almost touch my shins.

"Maybe he will."

"Maybe." He nods. He makes a show of thinking it over. "But not before he's completed his mission."

"What mission?"

Loren puts his empty beer bottle on the side table. "Look, Levi, you seem like a decent kid. And I know you care about your brother. But there isn't all that much you can do for him now. He's got some idea in his head, something he needs to do. I'm guessing you know him well enough by now to know that when he puts his mind to something, he follows through."

I feel my face go hot with shame. Loren is right. I'm not going to be able to convince my brother to come home, but it isn't this realization that brings the heat to my cheeks. It's the other realization: that this angry stranger knows my brother better than I do.

My shame morphs into rage.

I hate Loren.

I hate that Loren knows more than I do, and I hate the way Loren uses this knowledge to make me feel like a stupid child. But there's no escaping that what Loren has, I need—a different understanding of Boaz.

So instead of blowing up or storming out or any other of a variety of steps I could take at this moment, I ask him, "Does he seem okay to you? I mean really. Do you think he's okay?"

"I can tell you I've seen guys in a lot worse shape, and I've seen guys who are doing better."

I rub my fingers into my eyes. For just that brief minute I'm able to block out the world. There's nothing but a psychedelic blackness. I open my eyes again and watch the blackness begin its slow retreat.

"If I found him I'm not sure what I'd say. I don't know how to talk to him."

"Listen." Loren pulls in his legs and leans forward a little. "If you're going to keep on looking for him, I suggest you ditch the flip-flops and maybe pick up some camping gear, because the best you can hope for if you find him is that he lets you tag along. He's not going to turn around and drive home with you and your adorable non-girlfriend Pearl."

He gives my leg a friendly slap that stings more than it should. I know how weak it makes me look, but I rub the spot anyway. "Thanks for the advice."

"No problem."

We shake hands and I hold on for an extra beat.

"I mean it," I say.

"I know," Loren answers.

He walks us to the door. We start the climb down the narrow staircase.

"Hey, Levi," Loren calls after us.

"Yeah?"

"He likes to play cards."

"So?"

"Get him to play some cards. Do that, and you might get him talking."

ELEVEN

I TELL MY PARENTS I'm meeting Boaz on the trail. That he called from a small town in Vermont. That he asked me to join him. That he thought it would make for a good bonding experience. That he begged, pleaded: please would I bring along a batch of Mom's butterscotch brownies?

Mom responds by rushing out to buy me the same pair of boots Boaz settled on, then delivers a long lecture on the thickness of socks. How to avoid corns. Blisters. Rot.

Abba's response, not surprisingly, is to ask me what I plan to do about my job.

"You made a commitment to these people," he says. "You promised you'd work through the summer."

"Abba, the industry of in-home movie watching won't grind to a halt if I'm not behind the counter at Videorama. Everyone wants that job. Bob will find someone else."

"That's not the point."

"What is the point?"

"This is about commitment."

"Commitment," I say.

Abba's face softens. "*Motek*." He reaches for me. He puts

a hand on my chin. Tilts my face so he looks me in the eye. "Is this what you want?"

"Yes."

"I mean, is this what *you* want?" He places his palm flat on the center of my chest. "You? Levi?"

"Yes, Abba."

"Then you should go. Meet your brother. Walk with your brother. But make sure you apologize to the people at work. Let them know the circumstances are . . . extenuating."

"I'll do that, Abba. I promise."

And then: there's Dov.

"Bullshit," he says.

"Whaddya mean, Dov?" My face reddens. Among all the things I'm no good at, I'm a spectacularly lousy liar.

"This isn't right. Something's not right." Dov rubs the patch of wispy hair on his left cheek. He probably hasn't shaved in a week, but it makes little difference. There has never been a Katznelson man in the history of Katznelsondom who could grow a proper beard.

"What do you know from backpacking?"

He has me there. I've never been much of a nature lover. I was never a Boy Scout like Boaz. I am decidedly *indoorsy*.

I shrug.

"Why don't you tell me what's really going on," Dov says.

I start out by trying to dodge, but then it all comes rushing out of me like air from a little hole in a balloon. Faster and faster and faster.

Dov may be old, but he's quick, and he stays with me all through the tales of the maps and the Web sites and my suspicions and Loren with the scar on his forehead.

He nods wisely.

"When I was seventeen," he says, "I'd already met your grandmother. I'd have married her then if she'd have had me. Right then." Dov reaches over and takes my hand. He squeezes it. There's a decent chance he's shattering one of its lesser bones. "The thing is, Levi, I knew what I wanted."

"I don't think Mom and Abba would let me go if they had any idea what was really going on. Not that I know what's really going on, but you know what I mean."

"Levi, a few short weeks from now you could join the military. You could be walking headfirst into this godforsaken war. You're a man. If you want to do this for your brother, do this. Find him. Help him. Protect him. No apologies. No permission."

And with that we make a pact. Even though we don't say anything else to each other, Dov has just agreed to keep the truth from Mom and Abba. I've agreed to call Dov if somehow, somewhere I need the guidance of a real adult.

After I shower and run my toothbrush over my teeth with less effort than they deserve, I grab my bag and tiptoe down the stairs, careful not to wake my parents—it's early on a Saturday. But there stands Mom, in a long and wispy white nightgown, looking both ethereal, like a ghost, and impenetrable, like a linebacker.

Her back is to the front door.

"Don't go, baby. Please." Her eyes are damp. "I know you're not a child, I know. I know you can make your own decisions. I know I am . . . powerless over you. I know you have your reasons. But I'm begging you. I'm standing here begging you: please. Please don't go. Levi. Please."

Now she's sobbing.

I walk right up to her and put my arms around her. She feels like a collection of sticks inside a bag made from wispy cotton.

"Shhhhh," I say. "I'll be okay. Everything will be okay."

"No. Not you. Not you, baby. You. You are my baby." She weeps into the collar of my sweatshirt.

This time, the way she says that word, that *baby*—it doesn't annoy me, it doesn't make me cringe. Instead it turns my heart into an impossibly heavy brick. I almost have to sit down for the weight of it all.

"Shhhh," I say.

"No," she whispers. "No."

I take a step away from her. I adjust my backpack. I look down at my shiny new boots. My very first pair.

"I'm going hiking. I'm going to live in nature. Remember? Remember how great you said that was for you? Maybe it'll be the same for me."

"No," she says.

"I'll be okay," I say again, because I don't know what else to do but to lie to her. "We'll all be okay."

I slide her gently out of my way and walk out the front door.

. . .

Once again I've engaged the driving services of Miss Pearl Goldblatt. She's waiting for me, in her running car, outside my still dark house.

This time to New Jersey. This time to leave me behind.

It isn't until I reach the door that I see there's someone in the backseat.

Zim.

And he's pissed.

He's pissed that I started this adventure with Pearl. That I didn't ask him to come with us to track down Loren. That she had to call him and invite him along today. I didn't invite him, Pearl did. That's the real kicker.

He doesn't care that I came looking for him, that there's the missing skateboard to prove it. And he doesn't care that I'm going to recommend him for my job at Videorama. Zim hangs around all day anyway, I figure Bob might as well throw the guy a few shekels for his troubles.

But no. Zim is still pissed.

He won't even share his do-nuts with me.

Pearl gets on the highway, even though we don't know exactly where we're going. We don't know much other than where Boaz spent last night and where he's due to arrive in two days.

But at least, finally, we have some direction.

Turns out Loren is an ally. Despite first impressions, he's not this story's nefarious villain. He decided, after one or maybe ten more beers, that finding my brother maybe wasn't the worst idea in the world.

So he tracked down our home number, and luckily I answered, and he told me that things have changed. That the next address I had is no longer in play. The guy Boaz was planning on visiting, under pressure from his wife to cut ties with anyone and everyone having anything to do with the Marines, told him he couldn't stay there.

I erased that address right out of the Atlantic.

He told me that Boaz had camped in Harriman State Park and then last night he slept in a Motel 9 near Ridgewood, and from there he's headed to the home of a friend of Loren's landlord, someone with a kid in the Army, who wants to help Boaz out on his journey.

She lives in Edison, about two days' walk away.

I know it's a fool's errand searching for him now. It makes more sense to go looking tomorrow. But the need to get to my brother is whipping around inside me, and I don't really care if I do nothing but wander. It's better than sitting on the floor of my room doing nothing. So here I am, in a car full of fools.

Plus, we have the maps. Right now Zim is poring over them from his spot in the backseat. I've researched the most direct route that doesn't involve any major highway between where Boaz stayed in Ridgewood and the address of this friend of Loren's landlord in Edison. I have a list of every cheap motel and campground in between.

My brother is out there somewhere.

"I'm not only stronger than the two of you combined," Zim says as he shuffles through the stack of papers, "I'm also way smarter. And the only one without gainful employment.

So it really does boggle the mind why it is that I didn't come with you to Poughkeepsie."

Pearl has been given a two-day reprieve. Mama Goldblatt thinks she's driving me to Vermont to meet Boaz on the Appalachian Trail and that she'll stay and camp with us overnight before returning home. Zim told his parents something similar.

"We need equipment," Pearl shouts over the noise of the radio. "Spyglasses and infrared detectors and maybe we should have a whole new lingo to boot."

The sun is just beginning to break its way into the sky.

"We should have new names for each other. Code names. Double agent names. Names nobody would ever know us by. And speaking of names, what the hell kind of name is Loren for someone so downright scary?"

She's on her third cappuccino.

"He has a chick's name! And he's gotta be the least chick-like guy I've ever met! Loren! That's the name of someone you'd want to have over for tea!"

I rub the sleep from my eyes. I'll never catch up to the heights the morning's caffeine has taken her to.

"What about Suge Knight?" Zim asks. "He's about as unchicklike as you can get, and his real name is Marion."

"Excellent point, Richard."

"I aim to please."

I put my feet up on the dashboard and tilt back my seat.

"Don't even think about sleeping," she shouts at me. "That would be so totally unfair."

"I would never."

"Hey, I know. Let's talk about what you packed."

"Why?"

"For one, it'll keep you awake. For another, it's kind of like porn for girls."

So I tell her the contents of my backpack:

- 5 T-shirts. One from Pearl's convent. Two plain. Two with slogans on them. (WHAT IF THE HOKEY POKEY REALLY IS WHAT IT'S ALL ABOUT? and MEET MY PEEPS, under a picture of the marshmallow Easter candies.)
- 1 pair of running shoes.
- 1 fleece jacket.
- 1 lightweight rain poncho.
- 6 pairs of underwear, all boxers.
- 5 pairs of socks, brand-new.
- 1 pair of shorts.
- 1 pair of cargo pants Pearl tells me I look like a hobbit in but are nonetheless practical, not to mention comfortable.
- 1 ziplock bag assembled while deep in the throes of a hypochondriac's fantasy, filled with an assortment of pills, capsules, sprays, ointments, lotions and Band-Aids.
- 4 granola bars.

My cell phone and charger.

A folder stuffed with papers that Zim holds in his lap.

My wallet with $1,000 in cash slipped to me
    by Dov.
2 decks of cards.

"Nice work," Pearl says. "Except, of course, for the hobbit pants. But at least now maybe you can put those stupid pockets to some use."

"You lost me at the T-shirts," Zim says.

I've barely slept. I spent most of the night online, looking at maps. Taking the addresses Boaz had scrawled into the Atlantic and plugging them into search engines. My head is awash in satellite pictures—it's crazy the way everything looks the same from somewhere high up in the atmosphere. I can hardly tell Boston from Poughkeepsie from Edison from Baltimore from Washington, DC.

I know nothing much matters beyond the address Loren gave me—this friend of a friend. That's where I'll find Boaz tomorrow if I can't find him today. Once I find him, I won't need any maps, I'll be with him. But still, I couldn't help myself.

I wanted those addresses, those maps, those places seen from high above to tell me something. To whisper my brother's secrets. I beckoned to them: *Please*. But all I got in return was a lousy night's sleep.

TWELVE

By the time we reach Ridgewood, it's nearly eleven in the morning. We drive directly to the Motel 9, even though it's the one place we can be certain we won't find Boaz. He'll be long gone by now, but it somehow feels like the right place to start. Or maybe it's because it's the only place to start.

I walk into the lobby. I breathe in the scent of the cheap disinfectant. Over the years I've developed a nose for these sorts of things. I can tell the cheap stuff from the overpriced organic stuff Mom uses. I hear the sound of a vacuum from far down one of the long, dark hallways—a rumble barely masked by a Muzak version of "Yellow Submarine" pouring from the overhead speakers.

Poor John Lennon must be rolling in his grave.

I wander the perimeter of the small lobby. I finger the leaf of a potted plastic fern. I pick up a brochure for a local hot-air balloon company. I haven't seen much of the area yet, but can't imagine why anyone would want to pay $350 for the pleasure of observing this particular patch of New Jersey from the basket of a hot-air balloon.

I walk over to the front desk.

The guy behind the counter stands up. He doesn't look much older than me, although he has a thick mustache. Not that I'd ever grow a mustache, but I wouldn't mind the option.

"Can I help you?"

"I'm looking for someone."

"Name?" he asks, hands poised at the computer keys.

"Katznelson."

He taps quickly and then squints at the screen. "Checked out this morning."

"Yeah, I know."

He gives me a puzzled look and then seems to decide it isn't worth his time. He shrugs and sits back down in his seat.

I continue my path around the lobby's perimeter. From a small table next to an armchair I pick up a copy of *Women's Health* and then *Forbes*. I can't imagine Boaz reading either, so I put them both back down.

Pearl and Zim are sitting in the car. I can see them through the motel's glass doors. Zim is taking a nap. Pearl is on her cell phone. She looks up and sees me watching her. She tucks the phone into the crook of her neck and makes a gesture. *SO?*

I put my hands up in the air. I don't even know what it is I'm looking for, so how will I know when I find it? All I know is, I want to be somewhere my brother has been. To see something, hear something, touch something my brother might have touched.

It all feels so sad. So depressing. The few times I've stayed in hotels in my life, excitement crashed its way through me—I was *going* somewhere. I was on a journey. Some sort of special circumstance had taken me there, had led me to walk the unfamiliar halls, ride the carpeted elevators and sleep in the crisply sheeted beds.

But there's nothing special about this Motel 9 in Ridgewood. This is not a place that makes you feel like you're *going* someplace. There is nothing in here, not in the plastic fern, not in the stack of brochures, not in the three-week-old magazines, that brings me any closer to my brother.

The doors jingle as they close behind me.

"I gotta roll," Pearl says. Then she laughs. "I know." Pause. "*I know!*" Pause. More laughter. "Okay, later." She snaps her phone closed.

"Who was that?" I know it isn't Mama Goldblatt. She demands impeccable grammar. Despises slang. Prohibits the dropping of g's.

"Nobody."

"Nobody?"

"It wasn't nobody," Zim grumbles from the backseat. "Trust me."

"Okay. Fine. It was Il Duce."

"What!"

"Just get in the car, will you? Stop interrogating me."

I grab the folder of maps from Zim and climb in.

There are variables. Of course there are variables. Life is nothing but a whole mess of variables. But with all these printed maps on my lap, even though they only amount to a thickness of a few inches of paper, the variables suddenly feel one hundred stories tall.

The address Boaz is headed to, a house in Edison, is almost thirty-six miles from where we're sitting in Pearl's car outside the Motel 9.

So how to break down a thirty-six-mile stretch?

From all my earlier snooping, I know that Boaz looks at the road in twenty-mile segments, but now he has thirty-six to go in two days. Would he walk twenty miles today and sixteen tomorrow? Sixteen today and twenty tomorrow? Eighteen each day? Would the ratio look something more like a 22–14 split or any of the other ways you could break down those numbers?

Variables. Too many variables.

I pull a few sheets from the bottom of the pile.

These are maps of the ten-mile stretch that makes up the middle of this thirty-six-mile journey. Somewhere in here we'll have to go looking.

I've got a decent idea of the roads he'll take. I know he won't sweep far to the east or bend a western arc. I used a site I found in Boaz's browsing history that maps out the most direct route between any two points for someone who chooses to walk.

The way of the foot, as I've come to think of it.

"Where to?" Pearl asks.

I look at my maps. "The Oranges."

"Huh?"

"I don't know. Somewhere near West or South or just plain Orange."

"Okay. The Oranges it is."

We travel the driving route, not the walking route. It doesn't take very long. Twenty miles by car never does, and when we reach Orange I have Pearl drive another five miles south and we park in the lot of a CVS.

I figure it makes more sense to walk his route backward. That way we'll be walking toward him rather than behind him and maybe, with some crazy luck, we'll meet him face to face.

"So what time did he check out this morning?" Zim asks.

"I don't know."

"Don't you think that might help us figure out where he'd be by this time in the afternoon?"

Shit. I hate it when Zim is right. And Zim is right more often than he's wrong.

"I guess you need Pearl's spyglasses and code names and whatever because on your own, you're kind of a crappy detective."

Forty minutes into the walk and Pearl starts complaining. She holds her side and winces.

"You know, this isn't exactly a smoker's holiday."

We haven't made it very far. In part because I stop to look inside most of the businesses we pass along the way. Convenience stores, diners, sporting goods outlets.

I squint into the stuffy darkness of various bars. I search all the places Boaz might have stopped. I walk right by the hairdressers and nail salons and storefronts with names like Scrapbooker's Paradise.

Zim is really laying into Pearl about Il Duce.

"I mean, really! Are you totally incapable of having a platonic relationship with a member of the opposite sex? Even some pizza-faced yogurt guy? Does it always have to turn into *a thing* with you?"

"What about Levi? He's platonic."

"He doesn't count. He's Levi. He's like your brother. No, he's like *my* brother. He's more like your stepbrother. Anyway, he doesn't count."

"Right. And you don't count, Richard, because you're unattractive and dim-witted."

The afternoon is unseasonably cool. I'm wearing long sleeves for the first time in weeks. We've just come out the other end of an oppressive heat wave and I'm glad for Boaz, glad he's been given this break, because I can't imagine it's too pleasant to walk twenty miles or more in the kind of weather we've been having lately.

Then again, Boaz is no stranger to heat.

After walking a little over an hour it becomes clear it's time to turn back. I'm not quite ready to give up, but I don't want to drag Pearl beyond the point of no return. She's still keeping pace and bickering with Zim, but she's sweating and she's out of breath and I know her. Once she's had it she'll just sit down and refuse to move another inch, and I'm not up to the task of carrying her back to the car.

Also, I'm becoming convinced we've missed him. That our two points on the map have crossed. Maybe I underestimated him. Maybe he's already left South Orange in the dust. Maybe he's able to walk thirty-six miles or more on any given day.

We return to the parking lot of the CVS.

Pearl goes inside to buy something to drink and I sit with Zim on the hood of her car, looking through my folder. I'm scouring the list of campgrounds. It'll start getting dark soon and I figure we should settle in someplace for the night. Tomorrow we'll drive to Edison, to the address Loren gave me, and I'll . . . what?

Knock on the door?

Sit on the curb and wait?

Stand in the street and scream his name?

Tonight. All I can do is focus on tonight.

Pearl returns with an oversized bottle of some sort of water drink claiming healthy properties that can't possibly exist in a substance that shade of purple. She takes a gigantic swig, wipes her face on the sleeve of Zim's T-shirt and looks over my shoulder.

"I am *so* not camping."

"Why not?"

"The relevant question is: Why? Why sleep in the dirt? Out in the elements? I escaped a life of poverty in rural China by the skin of my teeth, okay? I will not go backward. I will not make my bed outside on the ground like a hobo when there's a hotel room someplace where a little hard-earned cash could buy us clean sheets and a moderately hot shower."

"I only have, like, a thousand bucks. I don't know how long it has to last and I don't want to spend it if I don't have to."

"I said *hard-earned* cash, Levi, so obviously, I meant mine." She reaches for her wallet. "Let's throw down some of my frozen yogurt fortune."

We find a motel with a lobby that looks exactly like the one I searched earlier that day near Ridgewood, although with a different name, and a dramatically superior sound track.

We check into a room with two double beds.

"This should be interesting," Zim says.

"Boys on one side, girl on the other." Pearl kicks off her flip-flops and starts jumping up and down on the bed to the left.

I feel tired. Defeated. Anxious. I feel all sorts of things that lead me into my backpack in search of my running shoes.

"You're kidding, right?"

"Nope." I tie double knots and do a half-assed round of stretches.

"Do you want me to go with?"

Zim is in pretty good shape. He's fast and agile, but I'm not sure he's much for distance. Not that it really matters anyway, because what I want right now is to be alone.

"No thanks, man."

He seems relieved.

Pearl flops onto one of the beds and turns on the TV. "At least have the courtesy to bring back some takeout."

I planned on running by the reservoir. Water is a place for me like the slope of my roof. Rivers. Oceans. Lakes. The pond where I walked with Pearl and Zim. Cheesy as it sounds, water is another safe place for me. I'm a decent enough swimmer, but really, what I like best is *looking* at water. Standing beside it. Gazing across its horizon.

I read someplace that the human body is sixty percent water. It makes perfect sense. Going to the water is like going home.

But despite all that, I turn away from the reservoir and begin running north. I don't have my folder with all the printed-out maps. I don't need it. By now I know the walking route by heart, and I start to run it in reverse.

It's a marathon, not a sprint.

Sometimes when I run, I hit this point, two or three miles in, where the act of running suddenly becomes effortless. "Runner's high," people call it. It has something to do with endorphins—which are, like, the same chemicals released during orgasm or something, though I can't say I see much of a parallel there.

Tonight I'm on this runner's high from the moment my shoes strike the pavement. My body is like this machine and I'm a bystander along for the ride. This body propels me forward.

It propels me north, away from the reservoir.

I've got four miles under my belt in no time.

I keep telling myself that I'm not looking. I'm only running. But I study each flash of a face, each blurry window. I glance in the bus stop shelters, even though I know full well that someone who won't ride in a car isn't likely to hop on a bus.

I forgot to pack my iPod. I'm not used to running without music. I'm not used to the sound of my own breath.

I decide to turn back when I reach the CVS, and when I do, just as mysteriously as it came on, my runner's high disappears.

I slow my pace.

That does no good.

I slow it some more. My lungs feel hopelessly small. My legs turn to dead wood.

Finally, I resort to walking.

It's night now. Full darkness. A stretch of quiet road unfurls itself in front of me. I miss my music. If I hadn't been raised on horror tales of the fate that befalls the hitchhiker, I might stick out my thumb.

I want to be in one of those two double beds. A pillow over my head to shut out the world.

Eventually I come upon a strip mall. I passed it on the way out, on the other side of the road. This time I notice, tucked in between a Hallmark store and an aquarium supply shop, a narrow and brightly lit Chinese restaurant.

It smells familiar. Where I am exactly I can't be sure, but this restaurant is this whatever-town's version of the Hungry Lion. Every town has one. That's why Dov loves the Hungry Lion so much. It reminds him of a place he used to go in Tel Aviv.

I've got nothing on me. No cash. No wallet. No cell phone.

But still, I walk toward it. Toward the upside-down duck carcasses hanging from the windows and the smell of fryer grease in need of a change. Toward the steam-warmed windows.

The place is half full, mostly with large Chinese families—

the true sign, I know, of a restaurant's quality. There are other people too. A couple of college-age guys. A white-haired woman and an even whiter-haired man.

And in the back, alone at a table with two empty bottles of Chinese beer, a head shaved close to the scalp.

THIRTEEN

I'M LIKE A JEDI MIND MASTER. I stand behind him using nothing but the force of my thoughts, willing him to turn around and see me.

Of course, he doesn't move.

And this I don't understand.

How can he not feel me standing here? How can he not know that I'm right here, standing behind him? Here, after all these miles I've traveled?

I'm scared of startling him or catching him off guard. I'm afraid to say his name. So I stand behind him and I wait.

Still he doesn't turn. He stays focused on the task of eating his perfectly divided dinner.

Rice. Noodles. Chicken.

There's an empty chair across from him and I ease myself into it. I brace for my brother's reaction. In this moment my own anxiety obscures my rationality, because my rational self knows that if I had a chance to think this through, I'd be able to predict Boaz's response, which is, of course, to have no response at all.

He looks up slowly. Catches my eye. And then he returns to the business of eating.

"Hi."

It's the stupidest thing to say.

Such an insignificant word. At only two letters and one syllable it's barely even a word at all, and yet, with an entire language from which to choose, this is what I say.

"Hi," he says. He reaches for a small bowl of wonton soup, raises it to his lips and drinks from it.

I feel the sting of tears come to my eyes, which is totally what I don't need right now. It's just that I'm so damn tired. So, so tired. But still. That's no good excuse. I swallow hard. The sting goes away.

"I've been looking for you."

He shrugs. "Well, you found me."

"Yeah, I found you in *New Jersey*."

"Yep. In New Jersey."

I stand up. I lean in close to his face and clear my throat.

The sting in my eyes is coming back so I bite the inside of my cheek.

"You," I say, "are an asshole."

My chair tips over backward with a loud clatter and I'd like to follow that move with an authoritative storming out of the restaurant, but instead my running shoes make a quiet squishing sound on the linoleum floor.

Outside, I pace the parking lot.

Outside, I let some of those tears fall.

I talk to myself. Mostly a string of expletives peppered with such questions as: *Why?*

And: *What am I doing here?*

And: *What did I expect?*

Your basic existential crap.

I sit down on the curb. I wipe my face on my T-shirt. I stick my head between my knees and take in some deep breaths.

I wait.

Which is really stupid.

Because he's not going to come after me.

That's for sure.

Because the truth is, I'm always the guy sitting on the curb. Or on the floor of my room. Or wherever. I'm the one who waits for something that never comes.

I let a few minutes pass. I let my breathing return to normal, and not that I spend a lot of time crying, but I've done enough of it in my life to know that my face tends to get a little splotchy. I give it some time to clear before I stand up and go back into the restaurant.

Boaz is right where I left him. He hasn't even bothered to pick up the chair. I reach for it, turn it over and sit down in it again.

I look at my brother and say, "I'm here."

"I see that."

"I'm not going anywhere."

"Okay . . ."

"I don't mean I'm not leaving this restaurant. I mean I'm here. I'm here to stay. I mean I'm going with you. Wherever it is you're going. Whatever it is you're doing."

"No. You're not."

"Yes. Boaz, I am. I'm here."

He's ordered another beer and he drinks from it as he looks at me. I look right back at him even though every fiber in me wants to look the other way. To study the crabs in the tank or the beautiful waitress lingering behind the cash register.

It's been only thirteen days since I watched him walk away, from the window of his room with the airplanes and planets still painted on the walls, but it feels like that day took place many lifetimes ago.

"I'm here," I say again.

Boaz reaches for his wallet. He looks over his check and then secures a stack of wrinkled bills under a half-empty bottle of soy sauce.

He stands up.

I think he's about to say something. He has that look of someone putting his thoughts into some sort of order. Whatever the order, I'll take it. Because something, any string of words from him right now, would be better than the nothing I'm so used to.

But then he turns and walks out the door.

This time I don't knock over my chair. I rise quickly and I follow him. Across the parking lot. Across the empty road.

"Go away," he shouts without turning around. He picks up his pace.

"Not a chance."

He takes a side street. Strides past a few apartment complexes. Turns right. Then left. Then right again.

I follow.

When I see the sign for the motel I feel this wave of relief. There was a small part of me that worried Boaz had, literally, taken to the streets.

It's a two-story motel with doors to the rooms that open onto the parking lot. Bo climbs a flight of steps with me on his heels. He reaches the door to room number 18. He digs into his pocket for his key card and swipes it. He opens the door and sticks a foot in the crack to hold it open, and then he reaches over and grabs me by the back of my neck. He wrenches my head close to his and he whispers with his hot, angry, beery breath, right into my ear: "Get the fuck out of here."

Then he shoves me away, steps inside and slams the door shut behind him.

By the time I return to our motel room—cold, hungry and rubber-legged—Pearl and Zim have fallen asleep. The TV tuned to some unidentifiable cop show.

They're on the same bed.

They're both in their clothes and on top of the covers and for both of those facts I am deeply grateful.

I make an effort not to wake them, but by her own admission, Pearl is a miserable sleeper. She shoots up and scrambles for her glasses.

She looks over at Zim asleep next to her.

"Oh my God. I slept with Richard. That is seriously *ewww*."

She hops over onto the other bed, and I sit at the edge in the not-quite-total darkness and tell her that against all odds I found my brother, in a strip mall Chinese restaurant, sitting at a table with empty bottles of Chinese beer and an equally empty face.

"How'd the food look?"

"Not the point."

"Right. Sorry. You know me and food. Please, go on."

I stretch out next to her and I tell her everything.

"He's in trouble," I say when I get to the end.

"We know. That's why you're here."

A long silence follows during which Pearl falls back asleep, her glasses askew. I remove them from her face and hold them in my hand, and I wake to the first hint of the morning light clutching them to my chest.

We head right over to the motel but Boaz has already checked out, which doesn't come as much of a surprise. We find a 7-Eleven and we drink our coffees and eat our do-nuts in the parking lot, on the hood of Pearl's car.

I lean back and close my eyes to the sun. I can almost trick myself into believing we're sitting out on the slope of the roof.

"So what's next?" Zim asks.

"Yeah," Pearl says. "What's the plan, boss?"

My head is swimming.

My neck is still sore.

I sit up. "Okay. Here's what I know. One: I know where

he's going tonight. Two: I know he doesn't want me going with him. In fact, I'm pretty sure he hates me. So for the sake of this list, let's make that I know he hates me number three. Four: I know he might change his plans for tonight simply to avoid seeing my face again. Five: I know I'll never find him if he decides to do that. And finally, six: I know this coffee tastes like doody."

I dump what I have left onto the concrete.

Pearl climbs down and opens up her driver's-side door.

"C'mon, fellas. Hop in," she says.

"Where are we going?"

"I don't know about you, but I'm sick of walking."

"You barely walked at all."

"Tell that to my calves."

"So? Where?"

"To eat a proper breakfast. With, like, protein and grains and all that. And later on, we'll deliver you to Edison and I'll go back to Frozurt and my puzzling flirtation with Il Duce. And Zim will go back to the life of a drifter unless Bob takes pity on him and lets him have your old gig at Videorama, but until then: breakfast. And after that, Edison. And in between: we're going to the movies."

The two-plus hours in the darkened theater, empty but for the three of us, does manage to distract me. Which is the effect I'm pretty sure Pearl was going for. I even doze off for a few minutes somewhere right in the middle of an extended action sequence.

When it ends, we stumble out into bright sunlight and damp air thick as Jell-O. The heat wave is back with a vengeance.

On the drive to Edison we keep mostly quiet. I let Zim ride shotgun. I'm remembering the trip to my first summer at sleepaway camp. Mom behind the wheel of the car I would eventually come to drive, the soft British lilt of the NPR reporter on the radio, the fat pines of northern Vermont, the yearning for home.

Unlike that summer, I now have the power to say: *Turn this car around.* Pearl will do whatever I ask. She is, after all, one of my two best friends.

I want to say it, to shout it, to grab the wheel right out of her unsuspecting hands, which are resting, in typical Pearl fashion, at ten and two o'clock. I want to wrench that wheel like Boaz did my neck. Turn it in the opposite direction.

But instead I stare out the window at the ugly stretch of gray interstate and I wonder how I'll get through this day. This afternoon. This evening.

This summer.

We stop a few blocks away from our destination.

Pearl turns off the car.

"I can go with you," Zim says. "For real. There's nothing much at home for me anyway."

"It's okay, Zim."

"I know it's okay, Levi. That's not what I'm saying here. What I'm saying is you're my friend. My birthday brother. I don't want you to have to do this alone."

"I won't be alone."

I'm not even sure I believe what I've just said but we let it hang there in the air between us.

"I think maybe Richard is right," Pearl says. "And you know that's saying a lot if I'm willing to admit when Richard is right."

"You guys. Thanks. Really. For everything."

I open the door.

I grab my pack from the trunk. I come around the side and lean in Zim's window.

"I feel like we're dropping you off at college or something," he says.

"Yeah, and he's totally embarrassed by his dorky parents so he's making us leave him a few blocks away," Pearl adds.

I stick out my hand and Zim slaps it.

"Peace out," he says.

I walk around to Pearl's side. She jumps out of the car and throws her arms around me. She squeezes hard. Then she hops back in.

"Try and avoid killing each other on the way home," I say.

"Try and avoid chafed balls," she shoots back, and then she peels out, because Pearl has never let an opportunity for drama pass her by.

I'm standing in the middle of the road.

It's one of those moments that feel like a big metaphor. You know those moments. The kind where the hero, not that I'm calling myself a hero, because if there's one thing we all know, I'm no hero, but in these moments the "hero" stands in the middle of the road. He can walk one way, toward the unknown and toward his fear. Or he can turn the other way and walk toward home and everything familiar.

But the thing is, this isn't a big metaphor, because in those moments there's a choice.

The hero must choose his path.

And for me, right now, there is no choice at all.

I walk the three blocks to the address Loren gave me. And I do what I know. I wait.

I sit out on the curb.

I'm facing what could be any house on any street in any town in America. Neatly trimmed hedges. Manicured lawn. There's an American flag hanging limp from a flagpole. In this perfectly still air it's got no place to go.

I wonder if there's a son in this house, another son who didn't join the army, a son whose job it is to mow this lawn. I wonder if this son still mows this lawn so that his mother doesn't have to hire the kid across the street.

I can't tell if Boaz has arrived already. If he's eating a home-cooked meal. Talking and sharing stories with a table full of strangers.

Or if he's still on his way. Still walking. Somewhere on the streets of New Jersey.

There is only one way to find out.

I ring the doorbell. A woman answers. She's got fire-red hair and a face like a slab of white marble.

"Bo," she says, and she reaches for my backpack. "I'm so happy to have you here. Let me take that from you. You must have had a long day."

I think back on the movie. The total lack of a plot and—except for a fantastic naked breast or two—the absence of any memorable moment. But that's not what she means by having had a long day.

I guess I can forgive her the mix-up. After all, I'm a complete stranger showing up on her doorstep with a backpack and hiking boots. But still. I don't look much like a marine. First there's the issue of my hair. And then, my less than worthy biceps.

I tell her I'm his brother. That I'm meeting him here. I offer to wait outside but she'll hear nothing of it. She whisks my backpack off someplace and returns with a can of Coke and a plate of cheese and crackers.

I learn that her name is Maria. That her son's been in three and a half years now. He enlisted on his eighteenth birthday. She's got pictures of him in uniform on every horizontal surface of the living room. There doesn't seem to be a father anywhere, but it's not my place to ask. Just photos of her son. Chin forward. Serious. Determined. The kind of face that's stock for these sorts of pictures, except for the galaxy of freckles scattered across his cheeks.

She tells me how lucky we are to have our soldier back.

I tell her I know.

Then the doorbell rings.

I try to keep a calm face. I try not to give away any of my panic. I don't want to be the cause of a scene inside this woman's house. She seems kind of fragile, and she's a good person. Just look at this cheese plate.

She goes to the front door and welcomes him with a hug. She leads him inside, over to me and the plate of cheese, and when he sees me he says: *Hey.*

Just *hey.*

All casual, like it's the most natural thing in the world to see me sitting here in this woman's living room. But in this *hey* there's a glimmer of respect. I've found him again, far away from where I found him last.

He says he'll take a Coke e sits down next to me.

"What do you want?"

What do I want?

What do I want?

I want to rewind the clock three years. I want him sitting on the couch watching movies with Christina. I want to hear his easy laugh. I want him to have done what every other high school senior at Bay State does—I want him to have chosen where to spend his next years from a list given to him by the sour-breathed college counselor, Mr. Hayes.

Or if not that, if he really had to become a part of this war that every sane person knew was a losing proposition, I want him to have gone and not lost himself someplace along the way.

I want to stop being angry at him for disappearing. I want to love him again. I want to help him.

"I want you to come home," I say.

"I can't do that now."

"Then I want to go with you."

Maria returns with his Coke.

"Suit yourself," he says under his breath.

She feeds us. She tells stories of her son. She's baked us a cake and I remember the night Boaz came home and how part of me thought we should have had one then, and I think of this cake as the negative image of that imaginary cake. This cake marks the beginning rather than the end of a journey.

She shows us her son's room, which has only a single bed, and she apologizes but says she was only expecting one, and anyway, it's all she has, and Boaz, in a voice so sweet I think maybe there's a ventriloquist hiding somewhere behind the curtains, tells her it's okay. He prefers the floor anyway.

She says good night. But then she stops and turns around and comes back into our room. She says she has one last thing to ask us.

"Will you pray with me?" she says.

And before we can answer she's dropped to her knees. We kneel beside her. She asks God to watch over her son. To watch over all the brave men and women who are so far away from home. To see that the troops successfully complete the mission on which they've been sent. She asks God to watch over the families who are waiting for them to return.

I'm not someone who prays. I've never asked God for anything, because I sort of figure there's no point. The only thing I got out of Hebrew school was Pearl.

I look over at Bo. Either he's praying hard too or else he's used to being around people who pray and he knows how to put on a good show.

I close my eyes and I give it a try. I don't know what to think about the mission. I'm not sure I know just what it is, so I can't go ahead and pray that the troops complete it. But there are other things I can try to pray for, I figure.

Please, I think. *Please let Maria's son come home safely. Let him come home the person he was before he left. Let him not close his door on her.*

She gets up again. Says good night for the second time. But this time she hugs Bo before she leaves.

I ask him if he wants to play some cards.

He ignores me. Not that I can blame him. It's a strange question to lead with after what just happened in this room, but I'm not so great with transitions.

He pulls a radio out of his backpack, plugs it in and sets it in between stations so that it plays only static. He takes the comforter off the bed and spreads it out on the floor.

We shut out the lights and in the darkness I want to talk to him and ask him one thousand other questions, but I don't.

I'm here.

He's allowed me to be here. I don't want to do anything that might disturb the magic of the words: *Suit yourself*.

When I wake up he's already packed and dressed and I'm pretty sure he'd have given me the slip if it weren't for his tripping over the cord of the radio and causing a clatter so loud it yanked me right out of a dream.

"Where to?" I ask.

"Get up and maybe you'll find out."

Maria gives us egg sandwiches for the road. From her front stoop she wishes us luck.

Wishing somebody luck implies there's something they're headed toward—a place, a situation, somewhere luck might come in handy.

Wishing somebody luck implies there's a destination.

A plan.

That unlike in the movie from yesterday, there's a plot.

We thank her for the food, the cake, the room with its single bed, though nothing we say strikes me as enough, and we say goodbye and we begin to walk.

Bo breaks a four-hour silence to ask me if I'm hungry.

I'm pretty much always hungry. You wouldn't necessarily know it from looking at me. But if you put food in front of me, no matter what it is, you can be pretty sure I'll eat it.

Zim is the same way.

We've talked about starting a reality show where we travel all over the world, to every obscure corner of the globe, and we eat whatever food people make us. We call our show *We'll Eat Anything*. Obviously there are kinks to work out. We could use a better title. And there's the matter of Zim's sensitive stomach. But the show would seriously kick ass.

So yes, I'm hungry.

We go to a diner. The sign just says DINER in red neon that looks like it's about to short out.

It feels great sitting down, even though I'm in the best

shape I've ever been. Some days I've run farther than we've walked, but something about the backpack, or the silence, has worn me to the bone.

We order burgers and milk shakes from a waitress who's insanely cute. I mean, crazy, crazy cute. She's got these shimmery lips and sparkly eyes. Her hair is held up on top of her head by a pair of chopsticks in a feat that seems to defy basic principles of gravity.

And yes, her tits are spectacular.

I invent a history for her on the spot. Home for the summer from a fancy college where she's on scholarship. The quiet type in high school. She's studying to be a molecular biologist. A poet, maybe.

"Anything else I can get you guys?" Her smile's a killer.

"No thanks," Bo says.

"All right then." She stands a minute, watching Bo, waiting for him to say more, to give her a reason to linger, but he's too lost to notice. She turns around and takes her order pad through the swinging doors into the kitchen.

Bo stares out the window. The gravel parking lot. The occasional car driving past. A crow on a fence.

It's hard to avoid talking when you're the only two people sitting in a booth.

"She's smoking," I say.

"Who's smoking?"

"No, I mean our waitress. She's hot. Don't you think?"

"Sure." He goes back to the window.

My cell phone rings. I hit ignore when I see it's Pearl. She'll be full of questions.

I shove the phone in my backpack and take out a deck of cards.

"Wanna play something?"

"Nah."

I start shuffling them. I do a bridge. Dov taught me how. We used to play this game called Knock-Knock, but it's been a long time. I can't remember the rules. All I know is Dov used to clobber me. He claimed to have the luck of the elderly on his side.

The crow on the fence has turned into a dozen crows. Loud and excited. Something heavy is going down in Crow Land.

Bo isn't even watching. He's looking someplace else.

"Check out that flock of crows," I say. "They're seriously pissed."

"It's a murder." Our waitress is back with our burgers. She puts the baskets down in front of us and takes a bottle of ketchup out of her apron pocket. "A murder of crows."

I think I'm in love.

"Right," I say. "I knew that. Like a gaggle of geese. Or a pride of lions."

"A sleuth of bears," she says.

She smiles at Bo again. This time he smiles back.

"So where are you guys headed?" She gestures to our backpacks propped up next to us in the booth.

"Ask him," I say.

"Where you headed, soldier?"

"Someplace," he says.

"Someplace like where?"

"Just someplace."

She still smiles but she turns the wattage way down. "That so?"

"Yep."

"Thanks for sharing." She drops the check on the table.

Maybe it would be better if Bo would just keep quiet.

FOURTEEN

FOR TWO DAYS WE DON'T DO MUCH other than walk. We have very little interaction with each other, or with anybody else—only the people who take our money in exchange for food, bottles of water and a dingy motel room with thread-bare sheets and ugly art.

When Boaz goes off to go to the bathroom or to take a shower or to run his electric clippers over his head, I take a look at my maps. It's useless. There's no answer in there. All roads lead to Washington, DC, or someplace near it, but I knew that already. What I still don't know is why.

I sneak a call to Pearl. I tell her I need her help.

She conferences in Zim, who's on the job at Videorama, which means he's sitting behind the counter not doing much of anything. She usually goes out of her way to exclude Zim, so there must have been something desperate in my voice.

While Zim's phone is ringing I ask Pearl how things are going with Il Duce.

"Whatever," she says. "I'm so over him."

"Hey, sugar," Zim answers.

"Hey, yourself," I say. *Sugar? Really?*

"Levi!"

"I thought I was sugar."

Is this really happening? Pearl and Zim?

"Okay, you two. Stop flirting," Pearl says. "Levi called because he needs our help. And as we know from all the great books and TV shows about dynamic trios, the job of the others is to drop everything when one espouses that particular sort of need."

"Speak English," Zim says.

"I think you mean to say *Speak English, sugar.*" I can't help myself. This is too much fun.

"Jesus, Richard. You really are a numbskull. *Espouses.* Not exactly a million-dollar word. *Expresses.* Levi is expressing the desire for our help."

"Oh, because I'm sitting here in front of a computer, and according to dictionary dot com, *espouses* means to adopt or champion, which makes what you said not exactly stellar English."

"Hello," I say. "I'm on this call too."

"Right," they say in unison.

So I ask them to help me with some research. Since I know where we're going, and I can guess roughly when we'll get there, I ask my friends to try to find out if there's an event, a meeting, a rally, something, anything of note happening in the greater Washington, DC, area within a week to ten days of when I expect us to arrive.

• • •

I finally get Boaz to agree to a game of cards.

Four slices of the pizza we ordered to our room are dead-weight in the depths of my stomach. We're seated across from each other at a table with a wobbly leg. The bulb in the lamp hanging from the ceiling is too bright for the moths. They dart around our heads instead.

"So, what'll it be? Your call." I shuffle and do my bridge.

Bo shrugs. "Whatever."

"A game of chance or a game of skill?"

"Aren't they all games of chance?"

"I don't think so."

Bo just looks at me.

"We could play Knock-Knock, but I can't remember the rules."

"Knock-Knock?"

"You know, that game Dov taught us."

"I've never played cards with Dov."

"Really?"

"Really."

I don't know why I find this so hard to believe. I guess I've always thought everything I did was because Boaz did it first.

"How about blackjack?" he says.

I do another bridge. This has got to be the most thoroughly shuffled deck in the history of cards.

"Okay. But you'll have to teach me how to play."

"For starters, we need a second deck.

"Good thing I came prepared." I grab the other deck out of my pack.

After several more minutes of shuffling, and bridges that are much harder to make look cool when two decks of cards are involved, I'm ready to deal.

"Let's go."

"Wait."

"What?"

"We need a wager," he says. "Something has to be at stake, or else what's the point?"

"Okay . . ."

"Your Red Sox hat."

"That's my lucky hat! Plus, it keeps the sun off my face and I'm trying to preserve my boyish good looks."

"Good. That means it's worth something to you."

He gave me that hat for my birthday six years ago. He probably doesn't remember. He probably doesn't even know it came from him. I'm guessing Mom bought it for me and slapped his name on the card. But anyway, I love that hat. So yes, it's most definitely worth something to me.

"So what do I get if I win?" I ask.

"You get to keep it another day."

We're talking, so I'm hesitant to actually start dealing the cards. Or to point out his lopsided rules.

Bo rubs his palms together. "Game on."

One round in and we realize our plan doesn't work. We need chips. Amounts to bet with hand by hand.

There's a bag of mixed nuts in Bo's backpack. We assign them value: ten points for cashews, five for almonds, one for peanuts. At the end of the night, whoever's got the most points gets the hat. Brilliant.

I go to grab the bag and when I do, I see the top of that Marty Muldoon's shoe box. The clown in his huge shoes smiling up at me. The place for all the special, all the secret things.

I reach in to grab it, to pull it out and ask what's in it, but I don't because we're about to play cards, and we're knocking on the door of having a good time, and we're hanging out together and he's talking.

So we play blackjack.

And in the morning, when we pack up to leave for another day of walking, because he is always better than me at everything we do, he's the one who keeps the sun off his face with my favorite, lucky hat.

I make a call to Mom while Boaz runs into a store to buy more water. I keep it brief and vague on the details because even after all the maps I've looked at the last few weeks I still can't say with any kind of certainty where the Appalachian Trail goes and where it doesn't.

I tell her we're having a great time. I tell her how I love being so far away from everything. How quickly I've adapted to the absence of all those things that make life more comfortable.

She asks me about big-leaf aster. We share a laugh. And I pretend I'm losing her before she can ask to speak to Boaz.

Here's something I didn't know before all this walking: the interstate sounds like an accordion. It gets louder and softer, louder and softer, depending on how far away you've strayed from it.

Boots on gravel sound like eating a bowl of Grape-Nuts.

Birds scream like children on a playground.

This is what I'd been thinking when it happened. Thinking about sounds.

There's no telling what Bo had been thinking. We hadn't talked in miles. We hadn't seen much either. There was nothing to hold on to out there other than your own thoughts.

Looking back on it, I'm guessing it had been some time since a car passed us. I didn't notice that then, though. Some things you stop paying attention to.

I didn't even hear it coming.

A white Toyota pickup passes on the left, and Bo takes a headfirst dive into the weedy, dusty ditch to the right. He doesn't even scream. He just dives, and he covers the back of his head with his arms.

When I run over to him he's breathing heavy. Sweat on the back of his neck.

"WHAT THE FUCK?" I shout.

My first thought is that the truck somehow hit him. Impossible. I was doing what Abba always did with me on our walks through the neighborhood, what he did to keep me safe—I kept to Bo's outside.

Then I think maybe someone threw something out the window that knocked him into the ditch.

I'm afraid to touch him. He just stays like that, breathing heavy, lying facedown.

"Are you okay?"

Slowly he turns over and lifts himself up into a sitting

position. He brushes the debris from his knees. Stretches his arms over his head.

"No."

"Is something broken?"

Bo puts his face in his hands and lets out a sound that's one part laughter, one part sigh of resignation.

"I'm afraid it's my motherboard."

FIFTEEN

"Bingo," Pearl says.

We're walking. I drop a few paces behind Bo, but that doesn't really give me any sort of privacy.

"What do you know?"

"A ton. About everything. I'm not sure you quite appreciate this about me, but I'm like an off-the-charts genius. But we don't have all day to explore the depths of my mental prowess. So I'll just tell you what I know about the calendar of upcoming events in our nation's capital."

"Go on."

"There's a dog show. It looks like a biggie. The Breeders' Association of North America."

"Pass."

"There's a premiere of a modern Danish opera."

"Pearl."

"Okay. Seriously, Levi, this was kind of easy. I'm not quite sure why you didn't think to go looking at this before, but I didn't think of it either, so I'll cut you some slack. There's a big march. A support the troops rally on the Mall. There's some country singer performing who we're supposed to have heard of and they're prepping for a massive crowd. I guess there's some bill in the works in Congress about cutting back funding to the military."

"Huh."

"You don't sound so sure this is it."

I'm not sure of anything anymore. It sounds plausible enough. Obvious, even.

But here's an idea that woke me in the middle of the night. That's often when my ideas come. It's like they're on a different sleep schedule than I am. I can't say it out loud to Pearl because, like I said, there's no privacy out here, no door to close. But here's my idea: maybe this is about Christina.

Maybe, after all, this long walk *is* for the love of a beautiful girl. Maybe he somehow knows she's here with her boyfriend, Max, and he's coming to reclaim her.

That. Or a support the troops rally. Both ideas sound totally right and impossibly wrong.

"So what's up with you and Zim?" I ask.

"Nothing."

"Whatever you say, *sugar*."

"Oh, Levi. You know me. I'm just a flirt."

"But this is Zim we're talking about here. You hate Zim."

"Didn't anybody ever teach you that *hate* is a strong word?"

"It's one of your favorite words."

"True. But did you know that Richard reads? I mean, he actually reads. Like, for pleasure. He's not a moron. He's kinda smart."

"Of course Zim is smart. And sort of deranged. And anyway, what about Maddie Green?"

"Levi, are you trying to stir up trouble?"

Maybe I am. Pearl is usually right about these sorts of things. I'm not sure why the idea of Pearl and Zim together would bother me. I love Pearl, but I don't *love* Pearl. And I certainly don't *love* Zim. I don't know. I guess maybe I'm just afraid that they'll leave me behind.

"No," I tell her. "I'm just messing with you. That's what friends do, and I'm just trying to do my job."

I'm getting an idiot's tan out here wearing sunglasses and no hat. White around the eyes, red everywhere else. I tell Boaz I need a hat.

"Then we'll get you a hat."

An hour later we pass a secondhand clothing store.

"Wait here." The bell tied to the door jingles as Bo shuts it behind him, leaving me alone out front.

I'm tired. Exhausted. Mom used to tell me that boredom is a state of mind, but I think it might be a physical state too. My legs feel bored from all the walking.

The door jingles again.

"Here you go." He hands me the new hat.

"You have got to be kidding."

"Nope. Put it on."

It's a canvas bucket hat with a wide brim and a green ribbon around the middle, printed all over in large pink roses.

"I can't wear this hat."

He puts it on top of my head. "If you don't like it, maybe you'll start getting better at blackjack."

· · ·

I'm pretty sure I know where we're going tonight. It's an address from the ocean: 314 Olive Street, Riverside, New Jersey.

It fits. It's the right distance from where we began. But I don't know anything about why this address. Why this destination.

Once we get to the block I don't need to look at the numbers on the houses, because it's pretty obvious which one it is.

We're faced with a small crowd gathered on the front lawn.

There may be only twelve people total, but twelve's a lot when they're strangers and they burst into applause at the sight of you.

Without turning toward him I can sense Bo tensing up. Some things you just know.

A banner hangs between the windows on the second story of this gray-shingled house. It's a large sheet, spray-painted red, white and blue.

WELCOME PFC BO KATZNELSON.

A man with ruddy cheeks and a tangle of white hair steps toward us. He's wearing the clothes of someone a fraction of his age. His name is Paul Bucknell. He's the father of someone from Bo's unit who's still overseas.

"Welcome," he says. He reaches over and runs his hand over Bo's head. Rubs it hard like he would his own boy's. "We're so honored to have you here."

He introduces us around to the crowd, mostly neighbors. Everyone's got a drink. The barbecue is fired up.

It's a party.

Before I know it I'm holding a plate with a burger, a pickle and a mayonnaisey mound of toxic yellow potato salad. I'm also juggling a red plastic cup of something fruity. I've got no idea if it's alcoholic or not, but I'm praying it is, because this scene is totally weirding me out.

Our backpacks have been whisked inside. A huddle of men surrounds Bo. It occurs to me that right now might be the perfect time to sneak a look inside that box from Marty Muldoon's. I could ask directions to the bathroom. Lock the front door behind me. Claim it's just habit. Track down the backpacks.

Open Bo's up . . .

My heart slams against my chest just thinking this way. I never got any sort of jittery heart when I used to go looking in his room.

I sit down in a chair under a tree. Take a deep drink of my fruit concoction. Inhale the fumes from the charcoal fire. Watch the crowd.

A girl in bare feet rides up on a bicycle. Hops off it and leaves it in the grass. She's got short brown hair. Cutoff jean shorts. White tank top. Big eyes. A silver hoop in her nose.

Paul throws his arm out and draws her close and kisses the top of her head. She pushes back against his embrace and wanders to the table. She pours herself a big cup of the fruit punch and downs it in a single shot, then wipes her mouth with the back of her hand.

She looks up and locks her eyes on mine.

I feign interest in my food. So caught up in pretending I

wasn't staring that I shovel a big spoonful of the potato salad into my mouth.

It tastes more toxic than it looks.

"What're you doing?"

She's standing in front of me.

I can't shake the sensation that she disappeared from the table and reappeared under this tree, that she burned a path from there to here, quicker than the human eye, like the Tasmanian Devil. All I know is that she's standing only inches away, her waist at my eye level, I'm balancing my plate on my knees, I've got a mouth stuffed full of potato salad and she's talking to me.

I man up and swallow the food. Wash it down with more punch. *Please, God, let it be alcoholic.* I'm in desperate need of a little false confidence right about now.

"I dunno."

"Oh. 'Cause it kind of looked like you were staring at me."

Busted.

"I was just zoning out." I can't decide if I should stand or not. Right now I'm looking up at her, and that feels sort of awkward. But what if I stand and I'm still looking up at her? That would be a whole lot worse.

She takes the chair next to mine.

"I thought it was funny. *You* staring at *me* when *I* look perfectly normal and you're wearing a hat like the one my grandma gardens in."

Oh Jesus. The hat. I whip it off my head and toss it under my chair.

I run my hand through my hair.

"So, do you know any of these people?" she asks.

"No."

"Then what're you doing here?"

"Apparently I'm embarrassing myself."

She takes my cup out of my hand and peers inside. Rattles the ice cubes around.

"You want more?"

"Is it alcoholic?"

"I doubt it. But I could fix that."

"In that case, yes."

"I'll be back."

She gets up and takes our cups into the house. A big sheepdog jumps up on her as she enters. She ruffles his shaggy hair. Gives him a good scratch behind his ears.

She returns quickly. Hands me my cup.

"So I figured it out," she says. "You're his brother. You're not another marine."

"How'd you figure that out?"

"The high and tight."

"The what?"

"The high and tight. The marine's haircut. You don't have it. And also, and no offense because I don't know you, but you don't look like Marine material."

"No offense taken. I'm Levi," I say.

"Celine."

"Like Celine Dion?"

I can't believe I just said this. I know from a lifetime of jokes about Levi's jeans that there's nothing more annoying than someone making an obvious joke about your name.

"Celine Dion. Good one. I've never heard that before."

A burst of laughter comes from the swarm around Bo. He cowers. Just a little. Not enough that anybody else would notice.

"That's your brother?"

"Yep."

"PFC Bo Katznelson?"

"He's the one."

She's pulled her tanned legs up onto her chair and hugs herself around the calves. Rests her chin on her knees. Her toenails are painted dark brown.

"My brother's PFC Mitch Bucknell."

I raise my plastic cup. She raises hers. "To Mitch."

For the record: plastic makes a disappointing sound when it clinks.

"He's supposed to come home for a leave in September, but I know enough now not to count on that."

"Yeah," I say.

If Zim were here he'd know how to talk to this girl. He'd be funny and sharp and he'd say more than *yeah* and he wouldn't get all obsessed with thinking maybe she'd mixed up their cups when she went to refill them and now he was touching his lips to the same spot she'd touched hers.

"So what's it like having him back?" she asks.

"I don't know yet. He wasn't really back long before he left again on this trip and I guess I'm still sort of trying to figure out who he is, like who he is now, and if that's going to be who he'll always be, and if that means we'll all always be different, and if that's the case, can that be okay."

I'm pretty sure I'd be making as much sense if I spoke to her in Urdu, but she nods.

Across the lawn a loud laugh escapes Paul and his ruddy cheeks turn fire red. He holds his side with one hand and the shoulder of the guy standing next to him with the other.

"He seems to be having a good time," I say.

"Yeah, he's getting his dose of testosterone. He's been missing that with Mitch gone."

I take the last swallow of my drink.

"How did your parents handle everything? Your brother's decision to enlist and all that?"

"Well, my parents are divorced, but that happened ages ago. My mom's kind of a hippie peacenik and the whole thing makes her uncomfortable, but my dad couldn't be prouder. It's like a big badge of honor around here, having a son in the military. And a marine! The elite of the elite!" She peers into her empty cup. "And I'm supposed to be uncomfortable about having a brother who's a marine when I'm visiting my mom and I'm supposed to wear my red, white and blue when I'm visiting my dad. But really? I just miss Mitch."

She grabs my cup from me and stands up.

"More?" she asks.

"In a minute," I say. Judging from how this first cup hits me, I'm pretty sure I won't remember much after the second cup, and so far, this is an encounter I'd like to remember.

She sits back down.

"What's your brother like when he comes home on leave?" I ask her.

"Tired. Hungry." She thinks it over. "Polite." She squeezes her empty cup until it makes a clicking sound. "He used to have a whole roster of names he'd call me, things like Butt Brain and Ass Wipe, you know, the basic stuff of older brothers."

Do I know? Do I know the basic stuff of older brothers?

"But now it's all *Celine* this and *Celine* that—he never used to call me by my name—and it's all *please* and *thank you* and it's like it's some sort of privilege to be hanging out at home doing nothing."

"I don't know about the privilege part, but I know about the tired part. Sometimes he sleeps for days. And he doesn't much like coming out of his room."

"Would you?"

"Would I what?"

"Would you want to come out of your room if you came back to it after so much time away? Months of living in the dust? Of people shooting at you? Of never getting a moment's peace?"

This sounds reasonable enough. It's probably how Mom sees things. Why she didn't do anything to intervene. But it's too easy, even for someone like Mom, who's looking for easy because the hard answer is too hard to face.

"Eventually you have to go back to life."

She points across the lawn to Boaz. "Looks like he left his room. Like he's getting back to life."

"Maybe."

She stands up again, an empty cup in each hand. "I figure I can't understand what Mitch has been through so I can't expect it to be like he never left when he comes back. And I figure if that means I have to live without getting called Ass Wipe anymore, so be it. And I figure . . . I figure you need another drink."

After the second round of Celine's fruit punch, just like I predicted, my head starts getting all swarmy.

Here's this girl sitting next to me, talking to me, so, okay, maybe she's talking to me because I'm the only person here remotely close to her age. But who cares? She's still talking to me and she smells good and she's got cool hair.

But the drunker I get, the less I'm thinking about her and the more I'm thinking about all the things I've ignored because I know Bo's life was hard over there, and I think of all the things I don't ask him because I'm too cowardly to face him and his high and tight.

So what do I do?

Do I march across the lawn and part the crowd and grab Bo by his T-shirt? Do I scream those questions right into his vacant face? *How could you leave us so completely? How could you hurt our mother like that?*

Of course I don't.

I excuse myself from Celine by telling her I need to pee, and immediately I wish I'd said *take a piss* because *need to pee* sounds sort of girly, and it's also . . . a lie, because I happen to have the bladder of a desert camel.

I stumble inside. I wander upstairs where there are closed doors, and I open them one by one, and my heart skips a beat when I see the Beatles poster in what must be Celine's room, and then finally I open a door to a room that has both of our backpacks on the bed. I reach into his, pull out the box from Marty Muldoon's and sit on the floor and put it in my lap. I stare at that clown.

And then suddenly Bo is standing in the doorway.

He doesn't say anything. He doesn't need to. His face, the room, the world have turned to ice.

Two big strides and he's ripping the box right out of my hands, and when he does the alcoholic clouds in my head part. With crystal clarity I know how seriously I've failed him. I know that Loren never would have gone digging through his bag. I know that he is a better brother than I.

"You looked like you needed help," he says. "I thought you were coming inside to be sick."

He shoves the box back into his bag and he throws the bag over his shoulder and he shuts off the light before slamming the door and leaving me in total darkness.

I don't even remember going to sleep.

But suddenly I'm awake and Bo's screaming and he's thrashing around on the floor and I wouldn't bet my life on it, but I'm pretty sure he's crying too.

I jump off the bed and I grab him. I try to shake him but I'm no match. He has me pinned in a blink. His hands around my throat. The back of my head hits the bare wood floor. A hollow thwack that makes my ears ring like church bells.

(*Maybe this is what it's like to wrestle with your brother*) I think. (*Maybe sometimes it goes too far.*) My brain tries to tell my body that's what we're doing. Just wrestling like we never did when we were younger.

But my body knows better.

He jumps back. Scrambles to his feet. Looks at his hands like they belong to somebody else.

I want to shout but instead I barely whisper.

"What the hell?"

He sits down slowly on the edge of the bed. Still breathing heavy.

His voice cracks. "I was dreaming."

I lie flat on my back. Rub my throat where he grabbed me. Touch my head where it's tender. Try to make some sense of where I am, how I got to this place.

"It was a dream," he mumbles.

"Some dream."

The night comes back to me in pieces.

Leaving the room. Finding Celine. More of her fruity drinks. Sitting with her under the tree long after the party ended. Never catching sight of Boaz again. Thinking maybe he'd left. Maybe he'd gone on without me. Not caring anymore. Stumbling onto the open lawn. Lying in the grass. The backs of my knees and arms itching. Not wanting to move. Not even to scratch. Celine next to me. Watching the stars. The earth spinning improbably fast.

I try sitting up. "Are you okay?"

"Yeah. You?" Bo asks.

"I'm all right."

"You sure?"

"Yeah."

"Sorry for that."

Without saying anything more we switch places. I go back to the bed and he goes back to the floor.

I'm grateful for the darkness of this room. Not even a crack of moonlight gets through.

"What are we doing, Boaz? What's all this about?"

It's not in a red plastic cup but in this darkness that I finally find my false confidence.

I can hear him shuffling around. Trying to remake his pathetic bed of cushions. He settles in. Goes quiet.

I try again. "Where are we going?"

There's a long silence that follows, but I hang in.

"There's something I need to do."

The box. What's in the box?

I only held it for a couple of seconds. It was heavy. Heavier than you'd think for a box built to hold the shoes of a child. I put it in my lap, without any thought, and before I knew it Bo was coming at me with a face made of ice.

"What do you need to do?"

"I can't tell you that."

I wish I didn't know about that stupid clown and his idiot's smile.

"You can't tell me or you won't?"

"What's the difference?"

"The difference is that I'm on this trip too, and it would help to know why I'm here."

"Why *are* you here?"

There are benefits to not knowing things. To never caring about anything. If I could turn the clock back half a night, I'd choose to keep my hands out of his things. I wouldn't have touched that box.

"I could go home tomorrow."

"Then go."

"Fuck off. Maybe I will."

I roll over and face the wall and pretend to go to sleep, even though I know sleep won't come. And I know that when tomorrow does, though I may not know where I'm going, I know where I won't be going.

I won't be going home.

SIXTEEN

I WAKE UP EARLY and I sneak outside to the front lawn, which is damp from the sprinklers, and I look through my folder for the letter from her, the one without the perfume and lipstick kiss, and I dial Christina.

It's six-thirty.

"Hello?" says a very sleepy and decidedly male voice.

"Is Christina there?"

"Who is this?"

"It's Levi. Tell her it's important."

The sounds of rustling sheets and whispers follow. Then the sound of feet on the floor and a door closing.

"Oh God, Levi. What happened?" She's breathing heavy into the phone.

"Nothing. Sorry. I mean, I'm not sorry that nothing happened, I'm sorry to call you so early, but the thing is it's hard to find a time when he's not around, and he's still sleeping, we had sort of a rough night, and I wanted to talk to you, because he's not hiking the Appalachian Trail, he's somewhere in New Jersey, Riverside to be precise, and I'm with him, and we're heading toward Washington, and I don't know why, but I'm wondering if it's really you we're heading toward."

"Slow down, will you? I'm still half asleep."

I breathe in the scent of wet grass.

"Did you break up with him?"

"What?"

"Did you dump him once he got over there?"

"It's more complicated than you're making it sound."

"Was it complicated? Really? Or did you just meet someone else?"

"Levi, what is this about?"

I sit down. I don't care if my clothes get wet. I don't care if the grass makes my skin itch. I see someone go running by, somebody about my age, enjoying a morning run.

"I guess I'm calling to ask if you think there's a chance he isn't over you. That he's trying to prove something to you with all this walking. Maybe he wants to win you back. Maybe he has something to give to you."

"Oh, Levi. I don't think so. I don't think you understand."

"I know I don't understand. I don't understand anything, and I certainly don't understand him. I don't know who he is anymore. Or maybe I never did. But I certainly don't understand who he is now."

A long silence follows.

"Listen, Levi. I want to choose my words carefully here, because I don't want you to think I don't care about Boaz, because I do, but he was my high school boyfriend. I'm not in high school anymore and neither is he. I know it seemed to you like nothing else mattered to us but each other. That's the myth of young love, isn't it? Or maybe it's not a myth, maybe it's true for a time. And you were just a kid back then, so I know that's how you saw us. As two people who loved each other until nothing else mattered. But other things mattered. Obviously, other things mattered more. He went his way and I went mine. And I still care about him, I do. I'll always care about him. But this isn't about me. I can promise you that. And whatever you may think, I don't know him the way you do. You know him," she says. "You know him better than I do, because I *was* his girlfriend, Levi. And you. You *are* his brother."

I close my eyes and see her butterfly tattoo. The royal-blue wings with purple swirls. Those wings begin to flutter slowly and I watch as that butterfly takes flight from her smooth, bare shoulder.

"I have to go," I say, and I snap my phone closed.

I find Paul and Bo in the kitchen, sitting at the table with coffee, a pile of toast and the local paper. I want to know where Celine is but I can't very well ask. It would come out sounding wrong. Or I guess it would come out sounding right—like just what it is. Like the way Zim sounds when he talks about Sophie Olsen. It would come out sounding like I'm hot for Celine.

I sit down and pour myself some coffee.

I think I hear footsteps upstairs. Is she awake? Will she come down and join us for breakfast? I could eat slowly, complain of a headache, find a way to drag out the morning so I can spend more time with her.

Or maybe she's not even here. Maybe she's gone by now. After all, she could have a job. Or a boyfriend.

"I might be able to think of some other folks who'd put you up. My sister lives south of here a stretch. Not too far out of your way. She makes a roast chicken that makes grown men weep," Paul says. "In fact, you should give me a copy of your route. I'll see what I can come up with."

Yeah, good luck, Paul. I'd like a copy of his route too.

"Sure," Bo says. "Thanks."

I stare at him with a mouth full of toast, but just then Celine arrives in the kitchen. I couldn't say if I smell her or see her first. Either way it's aces.

She's just out of the shower. Her hair is spiky and wet.

"Morning, honey."

"Morning, Pops."

She goes right for the refrigerator. Doesn't even look my way.

"You're up early. Going somewhere?" Paul asks.

"Yeah, it's my day at Mom's. So I thought maybe I'd do something kinda crazy and walk there." She takes a swig of juice right out of the carton. "With these guys."

Excitement whips its way through me like I've just hit blackjack.

"Honey, your mother's house is ten miles from here."

"Duh."

Paul is the kind of dad who thinks before he says no. I've seen the type. The opposite of Abba. Paul's the *I'm your friend* kind of dad. The *I dress younger than I am so I'm cooler than your dad* kind.

I can see him thinking it over. He's probably thinking that it's all fine and good to throw a barbecue for a marine he doesn't know, but letting his daughter wander off with one and his long-haired little brother is another story entirely.

"Dad. Mom's isn't out of their way. And anyway, I could use the exercise. I'm getting flabby."

So totally not true.

"Is your mother okay with this?"

"Are you kidding? Walking instead of filling the air with pollutants from my gas-guzzler? She'll probably want to buy me a pony."

Paul pulls his hands through his white hair.

"How about you guys? Okay if my daughter tags along for the day?"

"Yes," I say way too quickly. Crumbs fly out of my mouth. "I mean, sure. That'd be cool. Right, Bo?"

"Of course."

After we finish up breakfast Paul and Bo disappear to a room with a computer to go over our route.

"And a lovely morning to you." Celine is hiding behind the front section of the paper. She shakes the page as she turns it. "I trust you slept well."

If only she knew.

"I slept okay, I guess."

"You should thank me. I could have left you passed out on the lawn, but the sprinklers kick in at five-thirty. I took pity on you." She puts the paper down. Cocks her head to the side.

"You're funny," she says.

"I am?"

"Yeah. I would have sworn that you were going to kiss me last night. And then: Nada. Zip. Zero."

"I . . . I . . . I . . ."

I . . . need to do a lot better than this.

"It's all right, Levi. I've been wrong before. This wasn't the first time." She pats my hand. A friendly pat. With the flavor of condescension.

"So tell me. What does a girl need to do to properly prepare herself for a day's walk with you?"

"Well, you could start with some shoes. I noticed you favor bare feet."

"So you noticed something about me."

"Oh, I noticed."

She holds one leg out. Twists her foot this way and that. "I do have very attractive feet."

"They're not half bad."

"Shoes it is, then." She gets up from the table and I watch her walk out of the room.

I never figured leaving could be such a beautiful sight.

"So this is what it's like," she says.

"Whaddya mean?" Bo's up ahead a ways. Keeping his distance. I'm not sure if he's leaving me alone with Celine or just leaving me alone.

"I've never been on any sort of a political march before. I guess I thought it'd be a tad more exciting."

She has absolutely no idea how much more exciting this day is for me than any of the days before it.

"I'm not so sure this is any kind of a march."

"What is it, then?"

The question of the day.

"I'm . . . just keeping an eye on my brother."

I could tell her about the box. I could lean in close and let her in on a secret. We could hang back and whisper about Bo and wonder what he's up to, but I'm not going to do that, no matter how nice it'd feel to lean in close.

"Aren't you headed to DC?"

"Yeah."

"Why else do people walk to DC except as part of some political statement?"

"I don't know. I've never been."

This doesn't answer her question, but it does happen to be the truth. I spent the sixth-grade class trip to Washington, DC, home in bed with strep throat, and I never had occasion to go back.

I sent along a card to the president, bundled with those of my classmates, part of a pretty uninspired civics assignment. In it I thanked him for protecting our freedom.

I was only a kid. My world was different. Even the president was different.

But still.

We all have things we wish we'd never said or done in our lives, and among many regrets, one of my greatest is that folded piece of blue construction paper dotted in white stars affixed with the last dregs of a glue stick.

If I could have that card back, I'd shred it into blue and white confetti.

Celine grabs the bottle of water out of the pocket of my

cargo pants. (And Pearl thinks these pants serve no purpose! Ha!) She takes a long drink. It's hot out here. Very hot. And sunny. But there's no way in hell I'm putting on that flowered hat.

"Does he ever tell you anything? Anything about what happened over there?" she asks.

"No. Not at all."

"Mitch either. I try asking him, but all he does is tell me I don't want to know. Which is annoying, because if I didn't want to know I wouldn't bother asking. Then he just says I might think I want to know, but the truth is I really, really don't. So I don't ask him anymore."

"I don't even try."

"You don't even try?"

It isn't until she repeats this that I realize how ridiculous it sounds.

"I mean, I know there's no point."

"Except for the part where he knows you want to know."

"Yeah, except for that."

"Hey, don't beat yourself up. You're here, aren't you?"

I look down at her laced-up boots. I'm missing her bare feet.

"Listen. With Mitch I had to sort of relearn how to talk to him," she says. "How to relate to him. I had to stop being Ass Wipe and start being Celine."

"But do you recognize him? Does he treat you the same? Does he treat your parents the same? I mean, does he seem like the same person he was before he left?"

"Yes and no." She looks at me. "You think Bo is totally

different? Because a certain amount of different is unavoidable."

"He's different. That's for sure. He seems so lost. He can go through the routines, you know? He can show up to dinner and comment on the food and kiss my mom on the cheek when it's over, but sometimes I wonder why he came back at all. It seems he'd rather be anywhere but home."

"But he came home."

"Yeah, I know. I know he came home and we're all grateful. Of course we're grateful."

"That's not what I mean, Levi. I mean he came home. He didn't have to. He could have reenlisted. Or moved in with friends. Or started out someplace new on his own. But he came home. He . . . chose to come home. So he must miss you too and he must want . . . your help finding his way back."

Bo has turned into a dot. A small figure on the horizon. We've fallen far behind. There's no doubt that Celine slows me down, but I could do this all day. Forever.

Eventually we catch up to him outside a convenience store. He's been waiting awhile; he's taken off my Red Sox cap and he's sitting on the curb with a half-eaten sandwich and an empty bottle of soda.

I go in to grab some food for Celine and me. I don't know what she likes so I buy too much. I cover all the bases.

When I come back out she's sitting beside him and she's laughing at a story he's telling. It's a story about her he heard from Mitch. About when she was three and she'd gone to the mall with her family, and she'd wandered off during the scramble in the food court as everybody searched for something different to eat, and they didn't find her again for over an hour, and when mall security brought her back to her parents, she was wearing a scarf and sunglasses and carrying a purse, none of which belonged to her. She seemed surprised at how upset everyone was.

Where were you? they asked her.

I was shopping! she said.

"I've never been much of a shopper since," she says now. "I guess it's not as much fun when you actually have to pay for what you want."

There are too many things to count about this scene outside the convenience store that shock me:

He knows her. He knows something about her that I don't. He has stories. He remembers how to tell stories. He can charm people. He hasn't lost that. He's still able to make those around him smile. People can be with him and feel at ease. Unguarded.

Just look at Celine.

I stand there stupidly with my bags of too much prepackaged food.

"Your brother," Bo says. "He's a good man."

Celine laughs. "A man? He still has a pair of Spider-Man pajamas in his drawer and I know all his ticklish spots."

I spread out my purchases on the sidewalk.

"Your lunch is served, my lady." I do a little bow. "I've tried my best to cover the major food groups."

She eats more than I'd have thought possible, including

packing away three bags of chips. When she's done she dusts the crumbs off herself, stands and says, "Well, guys, I guess it's time for us to go our separate ways."

"But . . . we're going to take you to your mother's. This is a door-to-door delivery service."

"She lives another two miles east of here. I'm pretty sure you want to continue south."

"Door-to-door," I say again.

Boaz nods.

"How very chivalrous of you."

The two miles go by like two blocks.

Before I know what's happening we're standing in front of a town house.

"This is it."

"This is it?"

"Turn around," she says.

I'm afraid she's about to push me on my way without anything more. I have no idea how to do moments like this.

Bo pretends to study his maps. He's leaned up against a lamppost. She waves to him. He waves back.

"Safe journey," she calls out.

He returns to his studying.

She unzips my backpack and takes out my cell phone and flower hat. She turns me back to face her, then programs her number into my phone with her nail-bitten thumbs.

"I've already followed you over ten miles on foot." She hands my phone back to me. "Now it's up to you."

She puts my hat on my head. Grabs the wide brim with both hands and pulls me into her. She kisses me lightly. Way too quickly. Then she smiles.

"And win back your Red Sox cap, will you? This one doesn't go with your eyes."

SEVENTEEN

WE WALK UNTIL SUNDOWN.

We stop, finally, to spend the night in Philadelphia: the City of Brotherly Love. The motto comes from William Penn, the English Quaker, who imagined the area as a place where everyone, no matter his color, religion or background, could come and live in harmony and peace.

I learn all this from the motel pamphlet, which I'm reading for the second time, because Bo won't talk to me. In fact, our room is like a Quaker meetinghouse. Totally silent.

Some city of brotherly love.

"I'm sorry," I say.

Nothing. I wish he'd tell that story about Celine again. I wish he'd say something. Anything.

I get up from my bed and I go to the table and I take out the cards and I shuffle them. I do this because it gives me something to do. And I do it because I like the way the cards feel in my hands. I like the soothing sound of a perfect bridge, like running your finger over the teeth of a comb.

"I mean, you've got to try and see where I'm coming

from. I just want to know. I want to know what you're doing. Why we're here. Where we're going. I'm kind of flying blind. I don't know if you've ever been there. If you've ever been in a situation where you've not known what it is you're doing. It's not an easy place to be."

I take a few of the nuts we use for betting and I pop them into my mouth without thinking about it.

"So I'm sorry, Boaz. I'm sorry I went looking through your pack. I really am."

He gets up from his bed and comes over to the table, and he takes the seat across from me.

"Deal," he says.

I start whipping cards his way. I don't give him a chance to change his mind.

"I know what it's like to not know what you're doing."

"You do?" I ask.

"Yes. I do. So deal."

I wake to someone pounding on the door.

Bo's bed is empty, but I hear the shower running so I know it's not him.

Celine.

I throw on my cargo pants and run to the door and fling it open to find Zim and Pearl. He's got one arm draped around her shoulder and a large, wrapped gift in the other.

"Happy birthday, my birthday brother."

"What? How?"

Then I remember that Pearl was the last person I talked to before I went to sleep and I read to her from the motel brochure. In there somewhere it must have mentioned the name.

"Richard and I decided your eighteenth birthday warranted a road trip," she says.

"But? How?"

"Well." Zim's cheeks redden. "She came over last night at midnight. To, you know, be the first to wish me a happy birthday. And then we got to talking about you, and how my birthday wouldn't be the same without you because my birthday belongs to us, so we decided to come surprise you."

"Wow."

"Yeah. Wow. There I was, alone with a girl in my room at midnight, and I gave it all up for you."

"I'm the girl," Pearl says. "In case that wasn't obvious."

"Yeah, I get it."

"So happy birthday," Zim says.

"You too."

The funny thing is, I didn't even remember. So much of growing up you wait until the day you're eighteen, when the world sees you as an adult, and then the day finally comes, and I can't even remember.

"Come in," I say.

"We can't," Zim says. "We both have to be at work in six hours and it took us five and a half to get here."

"You're really going to turn around? Right now? You're going to drive all the way back?"

"Yep," Pearl says. "Luckily, there's good company."

She steps across the threshold to my room and kisses me on the cheek. "Happy birthday, Levi."

Zim hands me the wrapped gift.

"But I don't have anything for you," I say.

"That's all right. I'll consider you not giving me any shit about Pearl my birthday gift."

They look crazy happy standing on the threshold of my motel room. They're here. They've come all this way to see me. And I'm guessing they took the drive just to sit next to each other and to hold each other's hands. And I get that. Because I'd drive twelve, twenty, one hundred hours just to sit next to Celine. But also, they came to see me. I'm not getting left behind.

He gives me one of those guy hugs with lots of hard pats on the back and then I watch them walk down the stairs to Pearl's car. He has his hand on her elbow. I watch Zim open the passenger door for her. She climbs in and he walks around to the driver's side and starts up her car, and they take off.

Bo is still in the shower. He takes showers that last longer than the administrations of some small nations. I sit down on the bed and unwrap Zim's gift.

It's his skateboard.

Bo comes out with a towel wrapped around his waist and a puzzled look on his face.

"It's Zim's," I say. "I don't have one anymore. But we used to skate all the time. We lived for skating."

"I remember."

"Zim and Pearl stopped by and dropped it off for me." I turn it over in my hands. "It's my birthday."

Bo pulls on his clothes. He doesn't need to bother

toweling off his head. He doesn't have enough hair to hold water.

"I guess I missed a lot in the shower."

"Your showers last forever."

Bo sits down next to me. He spins one of the skateboard's wheels.

"I've gone a month without a shower. And even when there were showers to be had, you got in and got out 'cause some other guy was waiting. Often we were in old barracks that had no hot water, so contractors were hired to install water heaters, and sometimes they screwed up the installation, and there've been like twenty deaths from electrocution, where guys step in and get electrocuted just turning on the faucet. I never saw it happen, but it's one of those things you hear about. So taking a long, hot shower in a place where it feels safe to do so is maybe the best part of being back."

The wheel on the board stops spinning.

"So that's why I take long showers," he says.

"Thanks." I nod. "That's good to know."

"You're welcome." He makes a move to get up, but then he sits back down next to me. "Is this your worst birthday ever?"

"No, of course not."

"I'm not counting the one where the magician never showed and I threw on Abba's tie and tried to make a penny disappear up my sleeve and all your friends booed me."

I'd forgotten all about that. I was turning five.

I laugh. "That was worse. So was the one where we went looking for fossils."

"Yeah. The streets of suburban Boston are practically paved with dinosaur relics. I tried to talk you out of that one, but you'd have none of it."

"See? This is so not my worst birthday ever."

"Good. Because it's my best of your birthdays."

I ride on Zim's board, slowly so that I keep pace with Bo. This isn't a time for liptricks or ollies. I skate in a straight line. It sure beats walking.

After a mile or more of silence Bo asks, "Aren't you going to call Celine?"

"How do you know I haven't?"

"Just a guess."

"I will."

"It's your eighteenth birthday. Nut up."

He shoves me off my board and grabs it. He jumps on and pushes off so he's far enough ahead of me that I can talk in privacy—or at least as much privacy as one can get on the Baltimore Pike.

I flip open my phone. I scroll down to the Cs.

Nothing.

Apparently I don't know anyone whose first or last name begins with a C. In the space where *Celine* should be I find nothing.

Nada. Zip. Zero.

My heart sinks.

But I saw her. I saw her program her number in. She did it right in front of me.

Or was that just an elaborate ruse? Something she did to make it seem as if she liked me when really she never wanted to hear from me again?

I close the phone. Then I open it. I scroll down, starting with the As. I scroll frantically and then I find her. Right below *Demario's Pizza*. Right above *Dov*.

Dion, Celine.

I press send.

Smacked down, instantly, by the dreaded voice mail.

Beep.

"Hey, Celine. It's Levi. How are you recovering from the walk? I tend to feel it in my lower back, and I'm pretty used to this whole walking thing, so I can only imagine how your lower back feels. Anyway, that's why I called. To see how your lower back is doing and also the rest of you. Call me if you want. Or if you don't want you could still call me just to be nice. Because, like, it's my birthday, so I figure if you don't call—"

Beep.

Okay, so I tend to ramble. I don't know how to do the brief voice-mail message. I wish I'd thought it out more. Chosen my words carefully. But I don't really care. She left me her number. That's what matters.

I run to catch up with Bo. My brother, on wheels.

Five days: that's about how far I figure we are from Washington.

Six days: that's when the support the troops rally is scheduled to take place on the Mall.

Two a.m.: that's what time it is, and I can't sleep.

I stare at the ceiling.

And I get to thinking. All sorts of thinking.

I wait until I'm certain Bo is out. It's hard to get a handle on the depth of his breathing over the sound of the radio static, but I can see the steady rise and fall of his chest, so I'm pretty sure he's a goner.

I tiptoe out of the room in my socks and head to the motel's business center. Not surprisingly, it's deserted. For one thing, it's two in the morning. For another, who comes to this crap motel to do business?

I go online.

I read about the rally. It's a big one. It even has its own Web site: A Million Strong for America! I have no idea if that's a realistic number. Probably not. But maybe so. Maybe people are flying, driving, walking in from all across the country.

BRING YOUR FLAGS!! screams a banner across the bottom of the home page.

Could that be it? Could that be all the clown is hiding? A flag folded tight enough to fit inside a child's shoe box?

I search on. I read more.

Because while I was lying there not sleeping, while I was watching the digital numbers on the motel clock march toward daylight, while I was listening to the static and the faint sound of my brother breathing, I got to thinking about how little I've bothered even trying to understand.

I'm not pro or anti. I'm just nothing.

I'm just a nothing who can't sleep.

So now I'm sitting in the motel business center in the deadest dead of night, and I'm thinking, and I'm reading, and I'm learning, and I'm getting ready to be one of a million strong.

I'm getting ready to take a side.

EIGHTEEN

THE NEXT MORNING, finally, after all these weeks and miles and blackjack losses, I ask him the big question.

"Why not a car? Or a train? Or a bus? Why are we walking all the way to DC?"

"I just like walking."

I hop off my skateboard.

"That's bullshit," I say.

He doesn't stop.

"You can tell me." I holler because now there's a distance growing between us. "I want to know."

He doesn't say anything. I stand there with my board in my hands in the middle of another one of those moments.

I must choose my path.

I could turn around and ride Zim's old skateboard home. I could accept Bo's brush-off answer, let it go at that. Or I could catch up to him and make him see that I want to know. I really want to know. I want to know because I care about him and all this matters to me. He matters to me.

A couple of good kicks and I'm right beside him again.

"You take long, hot showers because they make you feel safe. I know that. You told me that and it's okay. Nothing terrible happened because you shared that information with me. So. Why don't you want to ride in cars?"

He doesn't look at me. He doesn't answer. He walks and I ride in silence, and together we cross the border into Maryland. I imagine at some point people fought hard for these borders. That these sorts of divisions mattered to somebody. But now you wouldn't even know you'd left one place for the next if it weren't for the sign welcoming you here and informing you that the state flower is the black-eyed Susan, the bird is the Baltimore oriole and the motto is *Manly Deeds, Womanly Words*.

"We were on the outskirts of this province in the north," he begins. "One of the more hellacious regions in that whole hellacious country, and we're rolling along, it's dusk, and you can't think about IEDs, because if you did, you'd never get in your Humvee in the first place, and IEDs can happen anywhere, anytime, and we know that, we've seen that, over and over again, but you just have to move ahead and take it on faith that you won't be one of the unlucky ones to make their acquaintance."

If it hadn't been for my late-night research session, I wouldn't even know that *IED* stands for improvised explosive device. Otherwise known as a roadside bomb. One of the goals of A Million Strong is to get more Cougars, which are like Humvees on steroids, and are a far better match head to head with an IED.

"So this one night we're rolling along, and I'm joking with my buddy about something stupid, and the next thing I know there's this big explosion as our Humvee and this IED are formally introduced. The whole fucking thing just blows apart. One minute everything is quiet, everything is fine, you can even let yourself have a laugh about something not worth remembering, and the next minute your friend is lying three feet away from his legs. And you check yourself. You feel your head, and you feel for your limbs, and everything is there. It doesn't even make any sense, but everything is there, and you're fine. And you look at your friend. And you look at his legs. And your brain doesn't let you comprehend what you're seeing, but you can't just pass out. You can't disappear into blackness. You have to do something. Say something. But what do you say to somebody who is lying three feet from his legs?"

His voice is shaking. The brim of my Red Sox cap is low over his face, so I can't see if he's crying, but I don't try to find out. I don't stare. One of the things about walking I always appreciated is the way you don't have to look someone in the eye.

"I don't know," I say. "I can't imagine."

"So if I don't have to get in a Humvee, or a truck, or a car, or even a train, if there's a choice, if I have a choice and I don't have to follow orders, if I can do what I want to do, and my legs still work, I'll just walk."

I step off my board and I tuck it under my arm and I don't get on it again for the rest of the day.

• • •

Tonight we're staying at Paul's sister's house. Otherwise known as Celine's aunt's house. You'd think that this connection might warrant a call back, but no. Leaving messages on Celine's voice mail is like mailing a letter to Santa Claus. I do it with as much hope and optimism as a little kid. And apparently I'm as likely to get a call back as that little kid is to get a handwritten letter from the big man himself.

But still.

I give it another shot.

And this time she answers.

"Hey, Levi, what's up?"

"Hey! Um, I'm just calling, um, again, because I'm on my way to your aunt's house and it, like, made me think about you."

Again: telephonic communication = not my strong suit.

"Where are you?"

"I'm in Edgewood. Two blocks from your aunt's house."

"How are you finding Edgewood?"

"It's lovely this time of year."

"Where are you now?"

"About a block and a half from her house."

"Keep me posted, will you?"

"Can do."

"I like you, Levi. Did you know that?"

"You do? 'Cause it's kinda hard to tell."

"Well, I do."

"Good thing, because I like you too."

"Now?"

"I'm on the block, I think. I just have to find the house."

"Two houses up on the left."

I'm looking up before fully understanding what she's saying, and there she is, on the front steps, in her bare feet, waving wildly.

"Hi," she says into the phone.

I still can't quite believe what I'm seeing.

"Hi," I say into my phone.

"It's good to see you."

"You too."

Bo hangs back and I take the steps until we're standing almost toe to toe.

"I'm going to hang up now," I say.

"Okay."

"And then I'm going to kiss you."

"Sure thing."

I think about all the times in my life when the minutes have passed like hours—Passover at the Schwartzes', Mr. Michaud's French class, Mom's trips to the department store to pick up new makeup. Why can't time ever slow down when it's convenient? When you want it to last forever?

After dinner, when everyone goes off to bed, I tiptoe down to Celine's room in the basement. I knock lightly. Hesitantly. The kind of knock I used to do on Bo's bedroom door.

It's past midnight.

She's still in her T-shirt and cutoffs. "You wanna come in for a drink?"

"What're you pouring?"

"I've got tap water in a glass with dried toothpaste on the rim."

I grab her and I step inside. I take her by the waist. I close the door behind me. Pause for just a second before I land my mouth on hers.

I expect a rush, endorphins, some sort of high, but what I feel instead is a total calmness. Peace. It almost sweeps the legs out from under me.

I pull back.

"So why didn't you return my phone calls?"

"I liked getting your messages. The way they sounded more and more desperate each time."

Girls can be so cruel.

"That's not very nice," I say.

I kiss her again.

"Maybe I'm not a nice person."

She kisses me back. Harder.

"I doubt that."

I pull her onto the bed.

"I knew I'd see you again," she says, kissing me more. "And anyway, talking is way overrated."

My shirt is already off.

I pull hers over her head.

I hold her against me. Her skin on my skin. Her chest pressed against mine. It's the single most amazing feeling in all of human history. Nothing has ever felt better, and I don't care if anything else happens, or if this is all there is, because I can't imagine anything feeling any better than this feels right now.

She pulls away. "So whaddya think?"

I prop myself up on my elbow and look her in the eyes. Try to catch my breath. "I think you're beautiful."

She is. She's so incredibly beautiful.

"I mean . . . should we?"

Should we have sex?

There's only ever one answer to that question, isn't there? Of course we should have sex. I'd be crazy to say no. But somehow, right at this moment, even though I've done little else but imagine some version of this for years, I don't care. For so long I thought having sex would change everything, it would make me a different person, a better person, a man. But now I'm here with her. And tonight that feels like enough. It still feels like one of those big moments without it being *the* big moment.

Plus there's the fact that with all that I've got in my hypochondriac's kit for bug bites, warts, blisters, splinters, fevers—I've brought along nothing for getting laid.

I run my hand over her shoulders, between the blades, all the way down to the small of her back. "Listen, Celine. I really, really like you. But . . ."

"But what? You're not ready to go to sleep yet? Because that's what I was asking about."

"Oh."

"You thought it was something else? You thought I wanted to have sex with you? You thought you're so irresistible that I was ready to throw myself at you and let you have your way with me?"

"Well . . ."

"Well, no, you big pervert. I was asking if we should go to bed. You upstairs in your room and me down here. Quickly before my aunt finds you here and calls my dad and he comes after you guns a-blazing."

"Right."

"So good night."

I stand up.

"Good night."

She smiles at me. She pulls on her shirt and stands up and walks me to the door. She blocks my exit. "But before you get out of here, don't forget my good-night kiss."

Dov wakes me in the morning. Six a.m.

I forgot to put my phone on vibrate.

He insists on meeting us tonight. In Baltimore. He's catching a flight and he's picked the restaurant. I tell him we're fine, that he doesn't need to come, but I know him. He wants to see for himself. He won't take my word for it that we're okay, or maybe it's that my word doesn't come out sounding all that sure, because the truth is, when I'm on the phone with Dov, I get this homesick feeling. I've never been gone from him long enough to miss him. Didn't even know he was missable, but he is. He's missable, and I'm sure he can hear it in my voice.

"I understand Baltimore is famous for its crab," he shouts. He still doesn't get that you can hear just as well on a cell phone as on a regular landline.

"And your mother. She's gone off the deep end with this Jewish *mishugas*. She's placed a ban on shellfish in the house. Shellfish! What did a shellfish ever do to her?"

So he's coming. And I have to tell Bo. I haven't even told him Dov knows we're not on the Appalachian Trail, or that I've been giving Dov updates on our trip the whole way.

And all of that's a big drag, but not as big a drag as it is having to say goodbye to Celine again.

A few short minutes remain before the house starts to stir. Before people get up and brush teeth and grind coffee beans. So I do what I can to make those minutes feel more like the minutes at the Schwartzes' or in French class or at the makeup counter in the department store. I do what I can to make those minutes feel like hours.

I tiptoe down to the basement, where Celine is still sleeping.

I climb into bed next to her, wrap her in my arms. I close my eyes and I hang on tight.

NINETEEN

I WAIT UNTIL THE LATE AFTERNOON to break the news of Dov's visit to Bo.

"Have you thought about dinner?" I ask him.

"Not really."

"There's a place I'd like to go."

"There is?"

"Yeah. It's a place for crab." I pause. "And Dov is going to meet us there."

That buys me about a mile or so of silence, during which I think of all the things I want to learn about Celine. All the questions I want to ask her. All the places on her body I'd like to kiss.

Finally I explain to Bo that I can't lie to Dov, I never could, that when I was leaving home I told him what I knew, which wasn't much other than that I was pretty sure the Appalachian Trail was a dodge. I tell him that Dov loves him and is worried about him and that he wants to see him, just see for himself that we're okay.

"Fine," Bo says.

He doesn't sound angry. I don't even get the sense that

I've flushed away whatever trust I've built up so far. I just get a whole lot of quiet, but that's something I know pretty well by now.

Dov is standing out front when we arrive.

He grabs us into a big bear hug and he kisses us both on both of our cheeks and it isn't until after all that that he notices my rose-covered hat.

"You're really taking your look to a whole new level."

"I'm doing my best, Dov."

I hug him again, absorbing the feeling of his strong arms around me.

He's brought a backpack. I know he doesn't own one, so he must have gone shopping. He looks like a kid on the first day of kindergarten. I can picture him in the store. Asking for a backpack like the one his grandsons have. I reach for it, to lighten his load, but he smacks my hand away.

We order way more than we could reasonably eat. Crab comes in every form. Fried, cracked, sautéed, lumped, cold, steamed. The only thing missing is liquid crab, but then I notice the crab soup on the menu. There is no crab territory left uncharted.

Dov wears a look of satisfaction. He stretches his arms out, resting them on the back of our booth. He sticks his gut out a little. Takes in the sight of us.

"You did this. You really did it." Broad smile. "What an adventure, walking so far. I admire you. Both of you. You've shown tremendous skill. Maturity. Conviction. I also hope along the way you've managed to have some fun."

I blush at this even though Dov can't possibly know that I've met a girl and held her naked chest against my own. He may know a ton, but he can't know everything.

He clears the plates from in front of him and leans forward. His huge forearms resting on the table. His face turns serious.

"And now it's time to come home."

Dov didn't come to eat crab. Of course he didn't come to eat crab. He's here on a rescue mission. He's come to Baltimore to bring us back.

"We're going to Washington, Dov." Bo stays calm. His voice strong and flat.

"Baltimore. Washington. What's the difference but a few hundred miles?"

"Actually, Dov," I say, "it's only about forty-five miles."

He shoots me a look. "Nobody likes a smart-ass."

The waitress approaches but then backs away slowly. Skilled enough at her craft to recognize when people don't want to be asked if everything is okay.

"Why not finish it here? Over an orgy of crab. It's as good a place as any."

Bo stares Dov down. For the first time ever, Bo actually looks bigger than Dov to me. "I can't do that," he says. "I'm sorry."

"Listen, *motek*. I know about war. Okay? *I know.* I've been there. I never had a doubt about serving, and there were times I even enjoyed being a soldier, but I deeply regret if I made it sound easy. It's still war. It's still ugly. It's still painful. But it fades. It does. Those memories, the things you've seen, they become like something from a book you once read, or somebody read to you, by a dim light, a long, long time ago. It takes a while, I know. That's why I thought this trip was not such a terrible idea. I thought it would give you the distance to close that book and start over again. You get a second chance. You can start over again. Like moving to a new house. Or a new country. Come home. Forget what it is you think you need to do. Come home. And let's start over."

Bo shakes his head.

I cover my face with my hands. It doesn't seem to hit Bo the way it hits me that Dov is pleading. I wouldn't have guessed Dov was capable of this kind of desperation, and watching it, I remember Abba and his naked body that day we fixed the fence.

There are parts of the adults around you you're never meant to see.

"There's a cab out front. It's taking me to the airport so I can catch the last flight back tonight. Come with me. Please."

"I can't," Bo says. "I won't."

Dov sighs. He reaches for Bo's hand and squeezes it across the table cluttered with empty crab shells.

"Okay."

He gets up and collects his new backpack. I walk him out to the street.

"Come back," I say.

"What?"

"In three days. There's a big rally on the Mall to support

the troops. A Million Strong for America. Fly down for that. Bring Mom and Abba. Let's all go together."

He puts his arms around me and I hold on for more beats than one of our regular embraces. He doesn't make a move to end it. That comes from me, finally.

When I pull back he studies my face.

"Look at you," he says. "Eighteen years old. A man." He reaches out and brushes the hair off my shoulders. Tucks a strand behind my ear.

"I'm proud to be your Dov."

I call Christina.

Parpar. The butterfly.

I don't tell her how the ink from her body still holds such a place in Boaz's imagination that he uses it as a lock for his secrets. What I say is that even though theirs was a high school thing, she's still a big part of his life. Of his story. Of who he was and who he is. Max or no Max.

I call Mom and Abba.

I call Pearl and Zim, which it turns out takes only one phone call, because aside from the hours she's serving frozen yogurt and he's eating popcorn at Videorama, they can always be found together.

I ask them each to come and be one of the million strong.

This doesn't have to be about the war, or what we think about it or why we're in it or what our exit strategy is shaping up to be.

I ask them to come here for Boaz.

I ask them to meet us on the Mall. Three mornings from now. So that he can see for himself that no matter how he feels in the darkness of his static-filled room, he is not alone.

On our last night before we reach DC I finally beat Bo at blackjack.

He throws my hat to me Frisbee style and I catch it one-handed and do a bow. At long last. My moment of victory. I put it on my head but it doesn't feel right. The shape of it has changed.

I fling it back. It belongs to him now.

He throws it back at me.

"You won it. You deserve it."

"No, it's yours."

"No, Levi. It's your hat. I bought it for you for your birthday."

"You did?" So Mom had nothing to do with it.

"Yeah. I remember we were leaving a game with Abba, the Sox won big that day, and outside Fenway you stopped to look in the window of one of those shops, and I saw you staring at the hat. And I said I had to go to the bathroom, that I'd meet you at the car, and I went into the store and bought it and hung on to it until your birthday. I think you were turning eleven."

"I was turning twelve."

"Right."

I put on the hat.

"And that was not one of my worst birthdays ever. It was definitely one of the better ones."

• • •

Our final day's walk doesn't bring us to the DC I've imagined since lying in bed with strep throat in sixth grade. No wide avenues or reflecting pools or cherry blossoms or white stone monuments.

Our final day's walk brings us six miles north of all that to the visitor check-in center at Walter Reed Memorial Hospital.

I hesitate before following Bo inside. I hate hospitals. I mean, who doesn't? Is there anybody out there who loves hospitals? Probably not. But I really hate them.

The guy behind the desk is in uniform. Bo stands rigid, but he doesn't salute.

"PFC Boaz Katznelson to see Staff Sergeant Jack Bradford."

We sit and wait. The room is filled with people not talking. I clean my hands with Purell from one of the many bottles lying around. I watch some CNN without the sound. Bo sits, chin up, back straight, eyes forward.

While we're waiting I start thinking maybe this is it. Maybe this is the destination. Maybe I've called everyone to meet us tomorrow at a rally Bo has no intention of going to. Maybe we came all this way to see Jack, to give Jack something.

Finally someone comes to get him. A woman in uniform. I settle in for what might be hours of silent CNN while I wait for Bo to visit his friend.

The woman looks at Bo, and then at me, over her clipboard.

"It's okay," Bo says. "He's my brother. He can come too."

I follow them both through a never-ending, complex set of stairways and hallways and walkways, past all sorts of doorways I'd rather not look into, until finally we reach Jack's room.

She steps in ahead of us, then comes back out and nods.

"Katznelson!" a voice bellows.

Bo goes right to his bedside. They shake hands and don't let go.

"You look great," Bo says. He does. Bo isn't lying. Jack's got movie-star good looks.

"And you look like shit," Jack answers. "But that's nothing new."

Bo introduces us. Jack repeats my name like it's a name he's heard before.

"Levi," he says. "Thanks for coming."

His roommate is home for a few days, so there's an empty bed we sit on while Jack shows off his legs. They're his third set, if you count the ones he left behind when the IED blew up their Humvee.

The ones he's got now are better than the ones the hospital first fit him with. Those made his stumps bleed. Now they're improved but still not perfect. He calls them his robot legs. He likes being upright, but they can't beat his chair for speed.

"The body is a puzzle," he says. "We're just trying different ways to make mine fit back together again."

Suddenly, I start to feel this itching in the back of my throat. Maybe it's exhaustion. Or the smell of the hospital. Or Jack's mechanical legs. Or just everything piling on top of everything else, like a stack of dishes that starts to list to one side before collapsing in a spectacular crash. Whatever it is, I'm about to lose it, and I know that the last thing I want to do right now is cry.

That's not what men do.

Men walk five hundred miles to visit a friend in the hospital.

Men walk for their brothers.

I look at Jack. He looks like Bo, who looks like Loren, who looks like the picture Celine carries in her wallet of Mitch. They are brothers.

Brothers don't get itchy throats and cry. They don't sit home on their bedroom floors staring at their toes.

They do something.

I get up. Bo has his pack propped up against the wall next to Jack's bathroom. He's too involved now catching up with Jack to notice as I reach into his bag. Quietly. It isn't the shoe box I'm after this time. I feel what I'm looking for and I grab it and I sneak into the bathroom and I lock the door behind me.

Bo's electric clippers.

TWENTY

"OH, SWEET JESUS," Jack says.

Bo just stares. Openmouthed. He's become a man of few words, but whatever he's got left in him, I've just snatched those away.

I rub my hands over my head. I don't think I got it quite right. I know I'm supposed to have a little more on the top than the sides, so maybe I don't have a true high and tight, but I am sporting an allover, super-short buzz cut.

Bo coughs. And then he starts to laugh. He turns red and holds his sides. He gasps for air. Jack is laughing too. They're hysterical. Tears flowing and everything.

And because laughter is more infectious than even the microbes I tried to Purell away, I start laughing too.

"Let's see it!" Jack says. "Bring us the fallen hair!"

I go back into the bathroom and collect fistfuls of my hair from the wastebasket.

"Man, you could knit my kid a sweater out of that."

"You have a kid?" I ask.

"No, but I will someday."

"Well, then, someday I'll learn how to knit."

· · ·

Visiting hours are over at nine, but Jack has some sort of a relationship going with the nurse on his floor. I'm not totally sure what sort, but whatever it is, he convinces her with his movie-star smile to look the other way.

There's an empty bed. And a pretty comfortable armchair.

"We'll get some shut-eye," Jack says. "And we'll take off before morning rounds."

"You're coming with us?" I ask.

"You got a problem with that?"

"No."

" 'Cause wait till you see how I roll. You won't be able to keep pace."

No matter how much it might feel like a prison here, this isn't a prison, it's a hospital, and Jack is a free man.

Technically.

But his doctors haven't cleared him to leave the grounds, and certainly haven't cleared him to ride in his wheelchair six miles into the center of the city. So we sneak out in darkness. Like we're doing a prison break. And again Jack relies on his friend the nurse, who helps to see that we make an unnoticed departure.

First stop: breakfast.

The waitress leads us to a booth before realizing that isn't going to work; then she gets all flustered and knocks over the chair she's moving to make room for Jack at a regular table.

He gives her one of his smiles and calls her darlin' and

tells her not to worry, just to bring us three hot coffees right quick.

As she walks away he says, "She must be new. 'Cause this place is a favorite hangout for guys in my condition. The press loves to offer us steak dinners if we'll talk about how shitty the hospital is or how screwed we're getting by the government or whatever, but I'm just working on putting the puzzle back together."

He looks at Bo. "What about you?"

"What do you mean?"

"What kind of shape are your pieces in?"

Bo doesn't answer, so Jack turns to me. "What kind of shape is your brother in, Levi? Like I said, the body is a puzzle. And the mind is probably the most complicated piece."

It's stupid, I know, because hair is hair and it doesn't say anything about who you are on the inside, and it doesn't change you, but sitting here with these two and looking like they do, somehow things feel different. I feel different.

"I think he could use some help," I say, and then I turn to Bo. "I think you could use some help putting the pieces back together."

He stirs his coffee and he nods slowly. "After," Bo says. "After today."

The morning quickly turns into afternoon. Yes, Jack is fast for someone in a wheelchair, but six miles is still six miles. I'd told everyone we'd try to meet up around ten, and we're already a few hours late.

228

I send a text to Pearl, my ambassador to the group: "On our way."

Pearl texts back: "No hurry. Million strong more like few hundred strong."

Me: "Hang tight. Have a smoke. See you soon."

Pearl: "I don't smoke anymore, douchebag. Don't you notice anything?"

Me: "What gives?"

Pearl: "Richard hates smoking. I like Richard. Do the math."

Jack seems to be having the time of his life. Which I know is a strange thing to say about a guy who's sweating bullets while using leather-gloved hands to push himself the distance of a 10k. He probably ran a 10k once to raise money for a cause, or as part of a neighborhood Thanksgiving ritual, or for any of the reasons people get together and run, and I'm guessing a guy like Jack did it in under thirty-five minutes.

But today it takes us some good time.

"Oh yeah!" he shouts through his heavy breathing. "Smell that freedom. It's a beautiful city and a beautiful world and it's just freakin' great to be alive."

Bo gives him a friendly punch.

"I mean, seriously. We can just cruise down the street here knowing that the trash in that Dumpster isn't covering up a bomb." He points one direction. "And we know that truck isn't carrying insurgents ready to open fire." He points across the street at a white Toyota pickup truck.

A white Toyota pickup truck.

Just like the one that sent Bo diving into that ditch.

"You saw a lot of those over there? White Toyotas carrying insurgents?"

"Sometimes Nissans. Sometimes with bombs in the back. The thing is, little brother," Jack says to me, "there's all sorts of stuff that in your previous life you'd never even give a second look, but this stuff, it's suddenly a trigger. Overflowing Dumpsters. White pickup trucks. I'm talking cold sweat on the back of your neck."

"Yeah," I say. "I get it." And if that sounds like a brush-off, it isn't.

I get it.

We take a break so Bo can run inside a convenience store and grab us some drinks. Jack asks for a beer. I figure the guy's earned it. And I've earned myself a Gatorade.

I look at my watch. It's one-thirty.

"How late do you figure this thing'll go?" I ask him.

"Who knows? Midnight maybe?"

"Midnight? And it started at ten?"

"No, it starts at sundown."

"That's not what the Web site says."

"What Web site?"

"A Million Strong for America."

"A million what?"

"Oh Jesus. That's not where we're headed? To the A Million Strong for America rally?"

"No. That's not where we're headed."

"Where are we going?"

"Your brother didn't tell you?"

"He doesn't tell me much of anything."

Just then Bo comes back outside.

"So where are we headed?" I ask him.

He throws an extra tall can of beer to Jack, who catches it in one leather-gloved hand.

"We're meeting up with some people."

"But not a million people?"

"I'd doubt that."

"We're not going to a rally to support the troops?"

"No, Levi. We're not."

"So? Where to? And you'd better tell me, because I have to go on ahead, but I'll catch up with you wherever it is you're going. I've come all this way—all this way, Boaz—and I think I've earned the right to know, finally, where it is you're going."

He looks at me, and just as I start to think this is it, that he'll give me one of those blank stares and say nothing at all, he says, "The Vietnam Memorial. At sundown."

"Thank you," I say. "I'll meet you there. You can count on that."

And I begin to run.

It takes me at least a mile before I remember I've got Zim's board tied to the outside of my pack. I grab it and I ride it a few blocks, but that doesn't feel right. It feels like a cheat. And anyway, I'm a fast runner. I think I can make better time on foot.

So I run.

Having no hair left is working in my favor. It's not falling in my face or hanging heavy on my neck. I'm lighter, sleeker, faster.

I don't need a map. I've been looking at maps long enough to know my way. The closer I get to the Mall, the closer everything around me looks to the Washington, DC, of my imagination. I take it all in, despite the sweat pouring down my face and into my eyes. It's muggy. And hot. But I don't slow down. I keep pace. I have everything on my back, it's weighing me down, but I run and I keep time.

I'm in the final stretch of the 10k.

It's a sprint now. Not a marathon.

I run down Fourteenth Street until it dumps me into the Mall. I turn to my left and I continue to run. I'm coming up on the Museum of American History, and there, just like I'd planned for hours earlier, sit Mom and Abba and Dov and Christina and Pearl and Zim, waiting. Gathered in a circle on the grass.

And as I get closer I see they're not alone.

Two other people fill out this circle. Paul Bucknell and Celine. I'd told her about the rally but I didn't expect she'd show up. But then again, Celine is the unexpected. My unexpected. She's huddled with Pearl and Zim and this makes me burst into a big goofy grin and here I am, approaching all the people in the world who matter most to me, and I call out, "Hey! Hey, everyone!"

I get closer and they look up at me but nobody makes a move. They're looking at me like they don't even know me. And then Mom screams out, "Levi?" and she scrambles to her feet and she's coming at me with Abba right behind her. It's then I remember my hair. Mom throws her arms around me and squeezes me and she says into my neck, "For a minute I thought you were Boaz."

"No, Mom," I say. "It's me."

And she's crying now. And she's squeezing me. And Abba is holding on too.

"I'm glad, baby," she says. "I'm so, so glad it's you."

TWENTY-ONE

THE RALLY ENDED HOURS AGO. Several hundred people packed up their several hundred flags and left.

We sit outside the Museum of American History on the Mall, littered with blue and red flyers, used-up water bottles and hot dog wrappers. A lonely worker in a green vest stabs the trash on a stick and shoves it into the large bag he drags slowly behind him.

I think maybe there's nowhere that feels emptier than a place still showing the signs of people who've already moved along.

I say what I can about the trip. I say what I can about Bo. I fill in what blanks I'm able, but still, there's plenty of blank space left.

Mostly, I sit in the grass and soak up what it feels like to be with my family again. To sit with Zim and Pearl. To look at Christina and think that yes, she's beautiful, but not as beautiful as Celine in her bare feet.

I lean over and whisper in her ear, "Thank you for being here."

Her smile is six miles wide.

I tell everyone that we'll see Bo later. At the Vietnam Memorial. I tell them that he's come all this way for tonight, though I also know that the old fortune cookie wisdom of the journey being the destination probably bears some truth here too.

I lean back and close my eyes to the fading sun. I sit up again and look around at the Mall and all the glorious buildings. I watch the lonely man in the green vest. He's hardly made a dent in all that trash.

I get up from the circle and I start to help him. Everyone follows. We all gather up those flyers and water bottles and hot dog wrappers because it's easier to do something than it is to sit around waiting for sundown to come.

We finally leave our patch of grass in search of food and discover a restaurant, where Abba orders a special bottle of wine. We toast Bo and Mitch and every man and woman who, for whatever personal reason, chooses to leave everything behind and put on the uniform of his or her country.

We walk to the Vietnam Memorial and by the time we get there it's already dark. We come upon a crowd gathered around a small stage. A birdlike woman with long gray braids stands under a weak lamp reading from a sheet of paper.

I look for Bo but it's hard to see anybody by this light and the people are packed in pretty tightly, so we just find a place at the edges, and we huddle together, and we listen.

She's reading from a long list of names.

When she gets to the end she folds up her list, but before she leaves the stage she leans in close to the microphone.

"And finally, James Eric Stanton, Jr. My only son. The kindest person I ever knew, and judging from how he kept his bedroom, the world's biggest slob."

She takes something from her pocket—too small to see from where I stand—and she kisses it and tapes it to the wall.

A college student follows her onstage, arms full of flowers. She reads a list of names and then talks about what they're doing on campus to raise awareness about the war.

This isn't a rally.

This is a protest. These people are gathered here to name the dead. They're reading a list of all the lives lost.

There's no flag in that shoe box he'd planned on waving with a million strong. He's come all this way to *protest*. He's *anti*.

Or is he?

Maybe he's come all this way to disrupt this protest. And he's got something with him to cause a disturbance, because he's not anti, he's *pro*.

Or.

Or maybe it's not a matter of one side or the other. It's not about *anti* or *pro*.

It's just about Boaz.

Maybe I should just stand back and listen.

Three more people take the stage to read names. Some leave notes taped to the wall. Some leave behind other objects.

The names pile up. One after the other after the other after the other.

As the next reader leaves the stage there's a pause, then some sort of commotion. Jack is trying to get up to take the microphone, but the stage doesn't have a ramp, so Bo and some other guys lift him to the platform in his chair.

Jack begins to tell the story I heard from Bo about riding in the Humvee and the IED, and it was hard enough to listen to this story the first time, when Bo told it, but hearing it again from Jack, from the one who found himself lying three feet from his legs, hell, that's even harder.

He reads the names of the marines who died that day, his brothers, he calls them, and he talks about how lucky he is to be here this night.

After they lift Jack down from the stage, Bo approaches the microphone and clears his throat. He has the box in his hands and he puts it on the podium in front of him.

He doesn't open it. He doesn't look at it. He's looking out into the crowd, but it's impossible to tell if he's looking at us. I don't even know if he can see that we're here.

"We were on checkpoint duty," he says. "This van comes barreling along. Too fast. A little reckless. So we fired some warning shots. You know, trying to get the van to slow down, but it doesn't. It's just flying. Only two weeks prior three soldiers were killed by a suicide bomb at a different checkpoint not too far away from where we were, so we knew not to take any chances, we'd been told not to take any chances and anyway, who wants to take chances?

"So there's this moment, this *what do we do* moment, but

the thing is, it's not really a moment, it's a collection of seconds and there isn't even any time to think it through because the van isn't slowing, so we do what we know we have to do, and we open fire.

"The van goes skidding off the road and flips over. And we go running at it, guns drawn. There's blood. Lots of it. And there's bodies. Everyone's screaming. It's total chaos.

"People are stumbling out of the wreckage. They're kids. Well, not little kids. But kids, you know, teenagers. And one guy gets right up in my face and he's covered in blood, it's all over his chest, it looks bad, and I know he should be lying down but he's screaming, just screaming, the same phrase, over and over, right in my face, and of course, I have no idea what he's saying.

"I'm screaming for an interpreter. I can't even remember if we've got one with us. Some of our guys are screaming that we need to take this kid down. He could have a gun, he could be strapped, he could blow himself up, but I'm thinking if he had those kinds of plans, I'd be dead by now.

"He's that close.

"He keeps screaming, the same thing over and over, and the guys in my unit are screaming at me *Take him down* and I'm yelling back at this kid: *I don't understand you.* But my screaming is just as useless as his, and I'm thinking about how fucking lousy I've always been with languages, but worse than that, I'm lazy. All this time in this place and I can barely say *hello*.

"Finally our interpreter runs up. Now I'm screaming at

the interpreter. *What's he saying? What's he saying? Tell him if he doesn't calm down and shut up he's going to get himself shot.*

"This poor guy's covered in sweat. He's a sweater anyway, but he just turns to liquid under pressure. He's talking a mile a minute to this kid, but the kid just keeps repeating the same thing, and he's clutching his bloody chest, and whatever our interpreter is saying to him just makes him repeat himself faster and faster.

"*What the fuck is he saying?* I scream.

"Finally the interpreter turns to me. He wipes the sweat from his face.

"*He's asking you to kill him,* he says. *He wants you to shoot him.*

"The minute this kid sees that I know what he's been saying, that I understand him, he stops and he looks at me. He says it again slowly. He pulls his hands away from his chest. He's not bleeding at all. He's clutching a shirt that's soaked in blood. He holds this shirt out to me and says something else.

"*My brother,* he says. *My brother is dead.*

"And again he asks me to kill him. One more time before he falls to his knees and sobs. And I get it. I do. Because I have a brother too."

I think I've forgotten to breathe for the entire time he's been talking.

Bo looks up and out into the dark, and he's still under that one light, it's shining right on him, into his eyes, but I'm pretty sure he sees me out here. That it's me he's looking toward.

And if it were just the two of us tonight, and if we were alone, and if he could hear my voice across this distance, I'd tell him that what he did at that checkpoint was heroic. He saved the life of that older brother. Anyone else might have given in to the panic, with everyone shouting to take him down, because he could have had a bomb, he could have been strapped. But Bo didn't do it. He didn't shoot him. He didn't kill him.

You didn't do it, Boaz. You saved that brother's life. You are a hero.

Bo takes the lid off his box and places it to the side. He reaches in and he pulls out a piece of paper.

"So the thing is," he says, "I don't know if it was me or not. It could have been, or maybe it was the guy standing next to me, or the guy on the other side of him. I don't know. I can't know. But I figure there's a pretty good chance I killed this guy's little brother or either of the other two kids in that van."

He unfolds the paper in his hand.

"So I've got some names I want to add to this list tonight. Three names."

He begins to read.

"Jassim Hassad, age sixteen. Tareq Majid, age sixteen. And Bashir Amar, age fifteen, brother of Wadhar Amar."

He reaches into the box and he pulls out a folded piece of fabric. It's not a flag, though for the briefest second I think that's what it is because I see a flash of white. But that white is just the small part of the shirt that isn't stained in the dark brown of blood that dried up months ago.

He takes the shirt and he places it next to the bouquet of

flowers left by the college student, as delicately as if it were made of sand.

He steps off the stage and someone else takes the podium. The evening's next reader of names. He walks through the crowd. It parts to let him pass.

He walks in a direct line right to where we stand waiting.

What follows are all the sorts of things you might expect at a moment like this. Long embraces. Some tears. Something like that night he slipped through our front door, unnoticed.

And then comes the pleading. Mom. Abba. Dov. Christina, even.

Come home. Boaz. Please.

"I will," he says.

"So let's go," Abba says. "Right now. I've brought the car."

Abba: forever the man of the practical solutions.

"I will," he says again. "But first I need to take Jack back to the hospital. And—"

"We'll give you both a ride."

I cut Abba off with a look. "Let him finish," I say.

"First I need to take Jack back to the hospital," he repeats. "And then I'm thinking I might stick around there myself for a while. Maybe try and get some help with all my pieces."

A long silence follows. Everyone else has stepped off to the side. Out here, in the dark, it's just Mom and Abba, Dov, Boaz and me.

I want him to come back as much as anyone. That's why I've walked all this way. That's why I went on this journey to this destination and all the others in between.

But I know, we all do, that by going with Jack, by going to that hospital and entering those doors and seeking out the help he needs, with this, he's finally beginning the task of coming home again.

"Come on," I say, and I throw my arm around him. "I'll walk you there."

ACKNOWLEDGMENTS

This is not the book I wrote: it is the book I rewrote. And rewrote. And rewrote. For this I must thank Wendy Lamb, my very patient and brilliant editor, who would, if I'd let her, strike a red pencil through the world *brilliant*, but as far as I understand these things, she cannot edit my acknowledgments. So there. I said it. She's brilliant. And I am forever in her debt. If I wanted to repay her someday, I might become an author who needs her less, but I don't see that happening anytime soon.

I also thank Douglas Stewart, my agent and dear friend, for his continued encouragement; his excellent advice, both personal and professional; his keen reader's eye; and his all-around fabulousness.

And more thanks:

To Seth Fishman at Sterling Lord Literistic. To Ruth Homberg, Catherine Sotzing, Megan Hunt, Kristen Rastelli, Colleen Fellingham, Barbara Perris, Stephanie Moss, Tamar Schwartz and everyone at Random House, especially Caroline Meckler, for all their hard work and help in turning this jumble of words into a book.

To my friends in San Francisco, and to the beautiful city itself, for making what was a difficult transition a wonderful adventure.

To my kids, who love to ask questions about what I'm doing on the computer all the time, and for whom I construct age-appropriate versions of whatever story I'm writing, and who are kind enough to refrain from telling me I'm boring them.

To Daniel, without whose love and support I could not write or do much of anything else.

And finally, to Markus Zusak, who is responsible in so many ways for what this book became. One of the greatest gifts to come out of my life as a writer is his friendship.

ABOUT THE AUTHOR

DANA REINHARDT lives in San Francisco with her husband and their two daughters. She is the author of *A Brief Chapter in My Impossible Life*, *Harmless*, and *How to Build a House*. Visit her at www.danareinhardt.net.